Breaking the Ice

Don't miss **YOU'RE INVITED**

by Jen Malone and Gail Nall

Breaking the Ice

Gail Nall

ALADDIN M!X

NEW YORK LONDON TORONTO SYDNEY NEW DELHI

ALADDIN M!X
Simon & Schuster Children's Publishing Division
1230 Avenue of the Americas, New York, New York 10020
First Aladdin M!X edition December 2015

Also available in an Aladdin hardcover edition.

For information about special discounts for bulk purchases, please contact Simon & Schuster Special Sales at 1-866-506-1949 or business@simonandschuster.com.
The Simon & Schuster Speakers Bureau can bring authors to your live event.
For more information or to book an event contact the Simon & Schuster Speakers Bureau at 1-866-248-3049 or visit our website at www.simonspeakers.com.
Cover designed by Jessica Handelman
Interior designed by Mike Rosamilia
The text of this book was set in Adobe Caslon Pro.
Manufactured in the United States of America 0216 OFF
2 4 6 8 10 9 7 5 3
The Library of Congress has cataloged the hardcover edition as follows:
Nall, Gail.
Breaking the ice / by Gail Nall. — First Aladdin hardcover edition.
p. cm.
Summary: Kaitlin has given up a lot—even attending school—to pursue her dream of being a champion figure skater, but after she throws a tantrum at a major competition, she is dropped by her coach and prestigious skating club and can only get a spot in the much-ridiculed Fallton Club.
[1. Ice skating—Fiction. 2. Interpersonal relations—Fiction. 3. Practical jokes—Fiction. 4. Family life—Fiction.] I. Title.
PZ7.N142268Bre 2015 [Fic]—dc23 2014013673
ISBN 978-1-4814-1911-6 (hc)
ISBN 978-1-4814-1912-3 (pbk)
ISBN 978-1-4814-1913-0 (eBook)

For my Evie Pea,
the reason for everything

Breaking the Ice

Chapter One

I have my fingers crossed for a gold medal.

Not where everyone can see them, of course, but hidden in the sleeve of my maroon-and-white Ridgeline Figure Skating Club jacket. If I win this competition, it'll show the judges I'm the skater to beat at Regionals in October.

My stomach rumbles. It's almost three o'clock, and the last thing I ate before I performed was a bowl of Toasted Oats cereal early this morning. And by morning, I mean even-the-birds-are-still-asleep morning. So by now, the concession-stand popcorn smells like something gourmet. I try to ignore it and stand on the tiptoes of my plastic blade guards to look for my friend Ellery. I can't spot her in the sea of girls in sparkling dresses crowding the hallway.

"Aren't you cold, Kaitlin?" Mom pulls her wool coat tighter around her.

I shake my head. I'm rolling back and forth on my blade guards. Heel. Toe. Heel. Toe. Mom and Dad got me new pink-and-white guards for my twelfth birthday, to match my competition dress. I glued some rhinestones to them, so they kind of twinkle in the lights when I walk. My coach, Hildy, always says you want every little detail to be perfect.

Mom checks the time on her phone. "Where are the results?"

Like magic, a competition volunteer threads her way through the anxious crowd in the hallway and tacks the results to the bulletin board. Everyone swarms forward. The volunteer has to elbow her way to safety.

A tingling feeling shoots through my body. This is it.

Dad squeezes my shoulder as we shuffle toward the board. Mom sips coffee and grips her phone, ready to post the good news online for friends and family.

Hildy keeps trying to guess who's placed. "It'll be a toss-up between you and that tiny blond girl from Detroit for first," she whispers. "It depends on whether the judges dock your double flip for under-rotation. The girl in the green dress from the Fallton Club was dreadful. She'll place last, for certain."

I tune Hildy out and squint at the eight-by-ten white sheet of paper. Ellery's in the very front. She hugs her mom, which can only mean she's gotten good marks. She's clutching the bejeweled pink water bottle I made her. It took me all day last Tuesday, but I finished one for every girl in the club, with their names in silver and tons of glitter to make them really sparkly.

Another girl runs off, her eyes red and watery. I can't see the names or scores yet, so I concentrate on not stepping on anyone's toes with my skates.

I'm not going to think about how the results of the Praterville Open can determine the course of my entire season and whole skating career. If I win here, then it shouldn't be hard to do the same at Regionals, where I can qualify for Nationals. Ever since I've known what Nationals is, I've wanted to go. And if I make it this year, I'll be on track toward the biggest competition of all—the Olympics.

Olympics. Just thinking the word gives me the shivers. Never mind that it's a few years away.

If I don't place well here, then . . . Right, not thinking about it.

"No matter what happens," Mom says, "you skated beautifully. And you deserve first place."

She has to say that. It's like a mom requirement.

"Can you see it?" Mom asks over my shoulder.

I look up, and there it is right in front of me.

Final Results—Juvenile Girls' Division. I scan the list for my name. I'm not first. Not second or third. My heart falls into my stomach. Not even fourth, fifth, or sixth. Maybe the judges made a typo and accidentally left me off.

But then I see it.

Eleventh place. Out of thirteen girls. Third to last. Loser zone.

"What?" Hildy's practically glaring at the sheet of paper. She blinks a few times, takes a deep breath, and then rearranges her face into a Professional Coach expression. "Well, I didn't expect that. Don't worry, Kaitlin. It's just a little summer competition. Not Regionals. Now where can I get a copy of those protocols?" She looks around like she's going to find an explanation of the judges' decision just lying in the middle of the hallway.

And it's not just a little summer competition. Hildy definitely knows that. Everyone knows that.

I stare at the paper. The number eleven glares at me. I run my finger across the page to my scores. I got a 22.35 for technical elements—jumps and spins and stuff like that.

That's a good score, especially this early in the season. Most of the other girls didn't even break twenty points. But the next column . . . 9.65 for program components, all the in-between moves, artistry and style.

"Nine point six five?" I feel light-headed. At my last competition, I got almost ten points higher. When the top girls in my group are getting nineteen or twenty points for program components, 9.65 is kind of pathetic. It's like the judges are saying my program was robotic. That I have no artistic expression, nothing interesting at all. That I'm boring.

I am *not* boring.

I know what I should do. I should smile and congratulate the medalists. I should wait until I'm safely inside Mom's car before I cry or complain or show what I'm really feeling. I should say I'll try harder next time. This is what I usually do when things don't go my way.

Dad puts his hand on my shoulder again, but I throw it off as I spin around.

"These . . ." I point at the paper. "These scores are a total joke!" What am I saying? It's like I'm not even in charge of my own voice. It comes out loudly and echoes down the concrete-walled hallway.

Right to the ears of the three judges walking past.

Mom's hand brushes my arm as my legs propel me toward the judges, who are stopped next to a table holding the competition medals. I stand right in front of them, hands on my hips. Words keep rolling out of my mouth before I can stop them, like they're coming from someplace deep down that I have zero control over.

"Did you even watch my program? I did a double axel! No one else did a jump that hard." This is *so* not like me. *Stop talking, Kaitlin! Stop, stop, stop!* "And I wasn't a robot! I had all kinds of style—and—and stuff between my jumps."

The judges blink at me.

It's like the words have a life of their own, and they're forcing me to speak them out loud. "My coach thought I'd get second, at least. But I guess double axels and choreography and . . . stuff are only good enough for eleventh place." Why won't my mouth stop with the words already? "I hope there are different judges at Regionals. Ones who know what they're doing."

For a few seconds, no one moves. I'm breathing so hard, it's like I just stepped off the ice after my program.

My mouth opens to say more.

No! I slap my hands over my face as if I can take it all back. But it's too late for that. I just broke one of the unwritten rules of competitive figure skating. The one that says Never Complain About Your Scores in Public. It's sandwiched right between Keep Smiling! and Don't Yell at the Judges—which I also broke.

I turn away from the judges. I can't look at them after I said all those awful things. Something tugs at my right blade guard as I take in the crowd of skaters and parents gaping at me. Mom's dropped her phone and hasn't even bothered to pick it up. Dad blinks furiously, like he can bat away the words with his eyelashes. And Hildy starts muttering things about subjectivity and sportsmanship.

I take a step toward them. I just want to grab my skate bag and get out of here. Something pulls hard at my right skate. What *is* that? I lift it up and—

CRASH!

The navy-blue tablecloth that was covering the medals table is now covering the floor.

"Kaitlin!" Mom cries.

Oh no. Oh no, no, no, no, no.

I reach down to unhook the teeny tiny, superhuman-strength thread from the tablecloth that had wrapped itself around one of the springs of my blade guard. My face is so warm, it's probably starting to match the color of my jacket.

My fingers are shaking, but I finally get the thread loose. I take a step backward to catch my balance.

CRUNCH.

Like this couldn't get worse. A glass figure of a skater in a perfect arched layback spin lies in two sparkling pieces under my skate. I vaguely recognize it as the centerpiece from the awards table.

"Kaitlin, don't move!" Mom says. She darts toward me and begins picking up the gold, silver, and bronze medals that dot the floor all around me.

The judges. They're staring at me. I can't look away. The big judge with the handlebar mustache clears his throat. The redheaded woman adjusts her glasses, probably hoping to see something different. And the tall, skinny guy reaches down and pinches the blue ribbon holding a gold medal from the top of his shoe.

The big judge huffs and shakes his head before they all walk off in the opposite direction. My entire body feels too hot, and I wish I were anywhere but here.

Dad gives a little snort, which turns into a cough when Mom shushes him. She gives him a look, and he springs into action, picking up medals from the floor.

No one else moves. Except a girl in a green dress—the

one Hildy said would definitely get last place.

"At least these aren't breakable," she says as she plucks a batch of silver medals from the floor around my feet. "Well, except for that glass skater. My mom would call it a dust collector."

I close my eyes and wish for a do-over. Of everything—my program, the scores, and my reaction.

"Kaitlin," Mom says in a cold voice as she rolls up the tablecloth. "Gather your things. We're leaving." Then she glares at everyone standing around, like she's daring them to say something. But no one does, of course. Mom's kind of scary when she's mad.

"Thank you," I whisper to the girl in the green dress. I can't look at anyone else.

While Dad fishes some cash from his wallet and slips it under the pieces of the broken glass skater, I grab my bag from the floor where I'd dropped it. Then I take off down the hallway, the skate guards snapping against my blades. Eyes follow me until I escape into the lobby.

Mom doesn't say anything else until we reach the parking lot. "We'll discuss this tomorrow."

And I know for sure she's really angry. I pretend to sleep during the long drive home, just in case she changes her mind.

Chapter Two

Saying a bunch of stupid words can't completely tank my figure-skating career, right? But I know there are some things you just don't say out loud in skating—at least not until you get home. It's not like normal sports, where everyone screams insults at everyone else, and no one really cares.

I didn't do it on purpose. That has to count for something. It all sort of just . . . happened. Instead of staying stuffed down like usual, the words fell out of my mouth before I could stop them. And pulling all those medals off the table was a complete accident.

I roll over and look at the clock. It's 10:02 a.m. I can't

believe Mom's let me stay up here so long. We got home from Praterville after midnight, and Mom disappeared into her bedroom without saying anything. I thought for sure she'd be up before dawn, in full-on lecture mode.

If I were braver, I'd go down there and get it over with. That's it. I'll go down in . . . five minutes. Or maybe I should call Ellery first, and *then* go downstairs. Except the house phone is in the kitchen, and Mom took my cell. Like that's a big deal. Ellery's the only person I really talk to anyway.

Okay. I'll clean off my desk. It's still covered in glitter and extra plastic water bottles from Tuesday. Then I'll read a chapter of *Little Women*. Or two chapters. I need to catch up on my reading. Then I'll go downstairs.

"Kaitlin! The kitchen. Now!" Mom's voice carries up the stairs and through my closed door.

So much for cleaning off my desk. I heave myself out of bed and pull my long light brown hair into a ponytail—just to put off seeing Mom for a few more seconds. Then I trudge toward the door and walk slowly down the stairs. I peek around the corner into the kitchen. Dad's sitting at the table, filling in the Sunday crossword puzzle. Mom's pacing with her phone in her hand.

"Sit."

I shuffle across the room, glad I'm wearing socks. The tile is always freezing, even in August.

"What do you have to say for yourself?" She leans on the table and raises her eyebrows at me.

Dad looks at his puzzle.

I gulp. "I'm sorry. I don't know why I said all that. It'll never happen again."

"What I don't understand, Howard," Mom says to Dad, as if I'm not even there, "is how so much rudeness came out of our daughter's mouth. Our usually quiet, respectful daughter."

Dad sort of shrugs and pencils in some letters. Mom's head swivels toward me.

"I'm sorry?" I look at my hands. Mom's right about one thing. I don't normally run around telling judges—or anyone—how I feel.

Mom makes a *hmph* sound through her nose. "You realize those judges will never see you the same way again?"

I nod. It feels like there's peanut butter stuck in the back of my throat.

Mom sinks into a chair, grasping her phone. And when she speaks, her voice is quieter. "Kaitlin, honey. This was so unlike you. I know competition is stressful, but you've always been gracious, win or lose. What made this time different?"

"I don't know. It just happened."

"Skating is your dream, right?"

I nod. It's the only dream I've ever really had.

"Do you understand how hard your dad works so we can afford to pay for lessons and competitions and skates? I didn't give up my career to homeschool you and take you to the rink and ballet lessons and costume fittings and competitions just so you could mess around. This isn't a cheap sport."

I nod again. I remember the look on Dad's face when he saw the thousand-dollar receipt for my latest pair of boots and blades. It was like someone had taken away his sports-channel cable package, stolen all the ice cream, and told him he could never crack a joke again. I glance at him now. He gives me a sympathetic smile.

Mom looks at me like she's waiting for more. When I don't say anything, she puts her Skate Mom face on again. "You owe your dad a hundred dollars for the figurine you broke."

Dad looks up from his puzzle and opens his mouth to say something, but Mom just keeps right on talking.

"You'll have to work extra hard to make up for how those judges might lower your scores in the future. And pray they don't mention it to other judges." She taps the corner of her phone on the table. "We have to do something to show you're sorry. You'll write an apology letter to each of them, telling them you appreciate the time they volunteer and that you are very, *very* sorry."

I know I shouldn't have reacted the way I did, but the judges are the ones who gave me such bad marks to start with. I think that makes us even. Plus, it's just embarrassing to write a note like that. But I'd never say any of that to Mom.

Although maybe I will write one to the skating club that hosted the competition. I feel really bad for whoever had to set up and reorganize the medals on the table I took out.

"Let's call Hildy and run it by her." Mom's punching numbers into her phone before she even finishes talking.

I cross my fingers under the table and hope Hildy will hate the idea.

"Hildy, hi. It's Laura. I have a thought. What if Kaitlin writes apology letters to each—what? I'm sorry, go ahead." There's silence for a few minutes, punctuated only by Mom's "uh-huhs" and "I sees" and Dad's pencil scratching away at the newspaper. Mom stands up and paces the room again, the phone to her ear.

"Uh-huh. I see." Each time Mom says this, her tone grows darker. This isn't good. I wonder what Hildy's telling her. Am I banned from the Praterville Open forever? Did I ruin everything for Regionals? If I can't place well at Regionals, I won't qualify for Nationals. And if I don't get to Nationals this year to start making a name for myself . . . My heart is in my throat. There's no way I can give up my Olympic dream because of one stupid mistake.

"Well, you need to do what you need to do." Mom drops into a chair and sets her phone on the table.

I look back down at my hands as soon as her eyes catch mine.

"That was Hildy," she says, as if I didn't already know that. "She . . . she's decided she can no longer coach you."

I jerk my head up. "But she's the only coach I've ever had."

"Apparently she's more concerned with her reputation than with an eight-year coaching relationship," Mom says with a sniff.

"But—"

"No buts about it. This is really a blessing in disguise. It's about time we looked for someone more advanced. More successful."

But I don't want another coach. There's a dull roar inside my head and a scream welling up in my throat. I stuff it down. My chest tightens, and I squeeze my eyes shut to keep from crying. I want Hildy. But Hildy doesn't want me. I can't get to Nationals without her cheering me on from the sidelines.

"Howard, what do you say to this?" Mom asks.

Dad glances up from his puzzle. He pulls off his glasses and reaches over to pat my arm. "It'll all be fine, Pumpkin. You'll see. This thing will blow over with Hildy. And if it doesn't, you'll get an even better coach."

I run the back of my hand across my eyes. "Do you really think Hildy will want me back?"

Dad nods.

Mom shakes her head. "No. I don't care if she begs. We're moving on. I'll talk to some of the other coaches at the rink in the morning. Maybe you can even get in with George Townsend. Now *that* would be a step up. Just think, an Olympian for a coach."

More tears slide out the corners of my eyes. I don't want George Townsend. I push my chair back. I can't sit here any longer.

"Grab a banana on your way upstairs," Mom says. "By the way, you're grounded for a month. No phone, no computer, no hanging out with friends."

I snag a banana—and a bagel when Mom isn't looking—and race up the stairs. Grounding isn't such a big deal. I don't know why Mom thinks it is. Doesn't she remember the last time I ever had anyone over? Two years ago. In fourth grade, right before I started getting homeschooled and all my friends probably thought I fell off the planet. I don't even hang out with Ellery outside the rink.

I chew on my bagel and open *Little Women* so I don't have to think about what just happened. The best part of being homeschooled is that you can have school in summer if you want to, and no school in December.

The worst part is that a lot of the time it feels like no one knows you're alive.

Chapter Three

I know something's off the second I walk into the rink lobby early Monday morning. It's just before five thirty, and everyone's talking way more than normal—until they see me.

I slink along the wall and pretend not to notice them. Mom's on my tail, like usual.

"Go ahead and get ready. I'm going to find George." Mom strides toward the coaches' room.

Ellery's warming up in a corner with Peyton, who's a year younger than us and one level behind. I leave my skate bag at my usual bench and join them. Peyton's kind of been attached to Ellery a lot lately. Last week they spent five whole minutes of practice time sitting in the bleachers and laughing before Hildy shooed them back onto the ice.

"Hey," I say as I start jumping up and down on the rubber-matted floor.

"Hey." Ellery's breath comes in wisps. She launches into a double loop—jumping up, turning twice, and landing gracefully in her pink-and-white sneakers. She doesn't say anything else.

Which is fine with me. I need to warm up anyway. We go through our jumps and sit, one by one, on the floor to stretch.

I look up from a straddle stretch to see Peyton staring at me. She smooths her coppery red ponytail and shifts her legs into the splits.

"So," she finally says. "Is it true? What everyone's saying?"

I stretch until my nose touches the floor so no one can see my face. Peyton's group had already skated, so I guess she missed out on the whole thing. "Yeah," is all I say.

"You really yelled at the judges? And threw the medals on the floor? You're the last person I'd ever thought would do that."

"I didn't mean to. It just popped out. And the medals were an accident." I'm still talking to the floor and hoping Peyton will quit asking questions.

"My mom told me Hildy dumped you," Ellery says.

I turn my head so I can see her just over my right knee. "Yeah." I can't say any more. My throat's all tight, and there's no way I'm going to cry in front of Ellery and Peyton. There aren't any secrets in a skating club. I should've known everyone would be in on what happened.

"So who're you going to take from?" Ellery asks.

I move into the splits. "I don't know. I think Mom's talking to George."

"George?" Ellery practically yells. "Seriously? Don't you have to, like, try out to skate with him?"

I shrug as I lean forward toward my knee with my arms over my head. "I guess I'll find out."

"George. Huh." Ellery jumps up and leaves me alone with Peyton.

"There's no way George is going to teach you. No offense," Peyton says.

My face goes warm. I've never felt so alone surrounded by so many people. Before Peyton can say anything else, I cut my stretching short and get up to put on my skates.

By the time the session starts, Mom still hasn't come out of the coaches' room. Maybe George really is interested in coaching me. I'd rather be with Hildy, but if she doesn't want me . . . George is better than no coach at all.

My blades make scratching noises as I move backward around the rink, and I realize I'm up too far on my toes. I shift my weight and the scratching turns into rhythmic, grinding sounds as the edges of my blades dig into the ice.

I catch up to Ellery, turn forward, and fall into step next to her. "I forgot to tell you Mom took my phone. Just in case you texted or something."

"Really? That's awful. For how long?"

"A month. Can you believe it?"

"Well, it is pretty serious. What you said to the judges, I mean. And everyone thinks you knocked that table over because you were mad." Ellery's looking straight ahead, her chin slightly tilted up.

"I didn't mean to say all that stuff. I don't know what happened. It just . . . came out." I turn backward again so I'm facing her. I thought Ellery would be more sympathetic, especially about the phone. After all, she's practically glued to *her* phone.

"I know. Only a crazy person would say something like that on purpose. You're a little weird, but not crazy."

I study her face for a hint that she's joking, but she's not smiling. What does she mean by weird?

Ellery's mom knocks on the Plexiglas that separates the ice

from the bleachers as we pass by. She's frowning and shaking her head. *Skate,* she mouths to Ellery. Ellery takes off without a word, moving fast around the rink.

Hildy glides onto the ice wearing her designer tracksuit and doesn't even glance my way. First thing Monday morning is my usual lesson time, but not anymore, I guess. Hildy stops on the far side of the rink next to Peyton. Looks like she nabbed my spot.

As I fly around the perimeter, I push thoughts of judges and scattered medals and Hildy and Mom away. It's just me and the ice. Me and the *scritch-scritch* sound of my blades. Me and freedom. The wind rushes past my ears, and I leap up into an axel, turning one and a half times in the air and landing backward on my right foot.

But no matter how many jumps I do, the thoughts come back.

"Kaitlin. Kaitlin!" My name echoes across the rink, loud enough that it drowns out the dance music playing on the loudspeaker. Loud enough that everyone looks around to see what's going on. Mom's bouncing up and down at the door, waving so hard I'm surprised her arm is still attached to her body.

I want to melt into the ice, but instead I skate as fast as

possible toward her. The sooner I can make her stop yelling my name and waving at me, the better. One time she did this at the mall, and the security guard told her she was disturbing the customers and causing a scene.

I skid to a stop and hop onto the rubber mats, just barely missing the toe of Mom's black ballet flat. "I'm here. What's wrong?" I try to grab her arm to stop her from waving, but she starts motioning all over the place as she talks.

"That's it! Take your skates off. We're leaving."

"What? Why?" I stare at her, trying to figure out what's going on, when the lobby doors open and Jennifer, the head coach, jogs out.

"Mrs. Carter, I—"

"It's Azarian-Carter," Mom says, nose-to-nose with Jennifer.

"I'm sorry. You have to understand, I need to act in the best interest of the club. Why don't we take this back into the lobby so we don't disturb the skaters?" Jennifer pushes one of the doors open and holds it.

I look from Mom to Jennifer. What in the world is going on? Mom glares at Jennifer and then stalks into the lobby. I follow her, thankful at least to be out of earshot of everyone else. I try not to look at the parents on the bleachers, watching us through the windows.

"How is it in the best interest of the club to lose a skater as hardworking and talented as Kaitlin?" Mom asks, hands on her hips.

Lose me? Where am I going? "Mom, I'm not going—"

Mom holds a hand up to shush me, and I shush.

"Kaitlin is a wonderful skater, and we hate to let her go," Jennifer says. "However, she broke club rules."

"Then make an exception. It was an accident. She was upset and didn't think before she spoke. She's going to write apology letters to each judge."

"I can't make an exception. The rule specifically states that disrespect toward any other skaters, coaches, judges, or officials will not be tolerated at this club. Period. If I make an exception for Kaitlin, I'd have to make one for every skater who breaks the rules."

Mom crosses her arms. "What about Hallie Dean? She cuts everyone off, even when they're in a program. How is that not disrespectful?"

So true. Hallie acts like she's the only person on the ice. If your program music is playing, everyone's supposed to move out of your way. But Hallie skates like her music is playing all the time.

Jennifer sighs. "That's a minor infraction. It's nowhere near what happened with Kaitlin. And the physical reaction . . . pushing over the awards table."

"She didn't push over the table. It wasn't intentional. Her blade guard caught the tablecloth, that's all," Mom says.

"That isn't what I heard."

They eye each other for a second.

"What's going on?" I finally get up the nerve to ask, even though I already know.

Mom shoots Jennifer the evil eye. "They're kicking you out."

My stomach lurches. Jennifer gives me a sympathetic smile. How can she smile and kick me out at the same time?

"But I've always skated here." My voice comes out as a whisper.

"Apparently that doesn't mean anything," Mom says before Jennifer can even open her mouth. "Just put your guards on and wear your skates to the car. We'll find another club. This is Michigan, after all. There are at least six within driving distance. More successful clubs than this one too. Any one of them will be thrilled to have a skater like you."

I race out into the cold rink and snag my guards and water bottle from the top of the boards, the short walls that circle the ice. I don't look at anyone, even though I feel them staring at me. Tears roll down my cheeks. I shove the rhinestone-covered guards on my blades and grab my skate bag from the bench in the lobby.

"And I expect a full refund on all the sessions I've paid for up front," Mom says to Jennifer before she grabs my hand and pulls me out the door into the parking lot.

A refund? Who cares about money? If I don't have a club or a coach, I can't practice. If I can't practice, I'm completely doomed at Regionals.

Chapter Four

While Mom repeats the whole awful story to Dad over the phone, I run up to my room. Crying into my pillow sounds really tempting, but it won't get me anywhere. Regionals are only a couple of months away. I can't miss any training time, and I *need* a coach.

Besides, if I'm busy searching for a new club, I can't think about what a mess my life is.

I scroll through the list of Michigan skating clubs online and click on the links to the ones that aren't too far away. I've heard of some of them from competitions. Finding one to skate at shouldn't be hard at all.

"Are you doing schoolwork?" Mom peers around the doorway to my room and squints at the screen of my laptop. "Remember, you're grounded. No talking to friends on the computer."

Instead of telling Mom she's completely deluded about my social life, I turn the computer toward her. "I'm looking up clubs."

Mom smiles and walks over to me. "I'm glad you're being proactive." She points to the screen. "Now *that's* a real club. Wouldn't you love to train with Joanna Michaels? She could get you to the Olympics."

I have no idea who Joanna Michaels is, but I just nod and say, "Yeah, that would be great."

She leans forward and clicks on a link that shows photos of the skaters. I scan the smiling faces, not recognizing anyone. Skating at a new club will feel like moving to a new town. I practically lived at Ridgeline, saw the same people every day, did schoolwork at the lobby café tables between sessions, worked out at the rink gym. And now I have to start over somewhere else.

Mom's sitting on my bed and has pulled the computer into her lap, clicking away and writing names and phone numbers on my pink flower-shaped notepad. I mumble something to her and walk down the hall to the bathroom. I wash my face and look at myself in the mirror.

"Everything's going to be just fine," I say to my reflection. "You're going to find a great club and a new coach. The coach will be so good, you'll blow away the competition at Regionals. Everyone at Ridgeline will be so jealous. You'll meet all kinds of new people."

I can't even think about the alternative—not skating at all. It's what I do every day. What I've done since I was three years old. Skating is like a physical need. When we go to Florida for a week in May, I do jumps in the surf while I count down the days until I can be back on the ice. Not skating ever again would be like cutting off a hand.

I force a smile at myself in the mirror, pull my ponytail tighter, and go back to my room.

"There," Mom says as she scribbles down one last name and number. "I'm going to call all of these clubs first thing tomorrow morning."

"Okay." I sit on the bed next to her. I'm not going to cry. Not, not, not.

Mom doesn't say anything. She just wraps her arms around me and squeezes. "We'll fix this," she says. "I promise."

And if Mom says she'll fix something, it'll happen. I smile and hug her back.

Mom clicks off her phone and crosses another club off our list. It's Friday morning, and I haven't been on the ice since Monday. I never knew it could take so long for people to call back. My feet are practically itching to put my skates on and do something. I miss the cold, and the sound my toe pick makes when I jab into the ice to jump. And maybe I'm going crazy, but I even miss the wet sock smell of the locker rooms.

Mom sighs. "Well, that leaves us one club."

"Which one?" I ask.

"Fallton." Mom doesn't meet my eyes.

"Oh." I don't know what else to say. I can't imagine telling Ellery and Peyton that I'm skating at Fallton.

"I know. It's not your first choice. But everyone else *claims* their coaches are all booked, or the club has a waiting list. But . . ."

I know what she's going to say. It's either skate with Fallton or don't skate at all.

"I want to skate," I say. "I just . . . well, everyone calls it—"

Mom cuts me off. "I know what they call it. I've heard the girls at the rink."

I bite my lip.

"Why don't we just go check it out? They've invited you to skate as a guest at one of their sessions tomorrow morning.

We can meet the coaches and some of the other skaters. We don't have to make a decision until after we've seen it." Mom turns her phone over and over in her hands as she says this.

I nod. That's reasonable. But I don't feel reasonable. Who wants to skate for a club that everyone calls Fall Down?

Chapter Five

It's seven a.m. on Saturday, and I'm curled up in the front seat of Mom's car, on my way to skate at the Fallton Club.

It's like a part of me has been missing all week, and I'm going to find it today on the ice. But then again, it's the Fall Down Club. The worst club in the history of all skating clubs. I can hear Ellery giggling in my head. *You're skating at Fall Down? Wow, Kaitlin, that's such a loser rink.*

Mom makes a left turn onto the highway. "We'll just try it out."

"Their skaters aren't very good." I feel bad saying this, but it's true. I'm thinking of the girl at the Praterville Open—the really nice one in the green dress who helped me. She placed dead last in our level. Her program music was this awful screechy violin stuff, and she fell three times.

"If we decide you'll skate there, I'll make sure you don't get whoever coached that girl at Praterville," Mom says, reading my mind.

I lean back in the seat and breathe in the citrus scent from the air freshener dangling from the rearview mirror. Mom claims it reminds her of vacations in Florida, but it smells like bathroom cleaner to me.

The drive to Fallton is only thirty minutes, but it feels even shorter than that. Before I know it, we're parked outside the rink.

I get out of the car and smooth my clothes. It took me forever to decide what to wear. At my old club, skaters wore either plain practice dresses or tight skating pants. I put on my favorite black dress this morning but took it off. I didn't want to look overdressed if everyone else was wearing pants. So I went with my black pants with the white stripes down the sides.

Mom pushes open the door, and we walk down a short, narrow hallway to the lobby. It's way smaller than my old rink. Straight across from us, rough white ice shows through the windows that line the far side of the lobby. An ancient, dirty, rusty Zamboni chugs around in slow circles, smoothing the ice and sending fumes throughout the building. I wrinkle my nose and try not to breathe too deeply.

The bathrooms are off to the right, along with an open door with a sign hanging over it that reads LOCKER ROOMS. The *L* dangles from the sign at an angle that makes it look like a *V*. Vocker Rooms. I bite my lip to keep from giggling.

Then I remember this is my new rink. Not new, shiny, so-white-it-glows Ridgeline Ice Plex, but this place—Vocker Rooms and all.

Rows of dull orange plastic chairs are scattered throughout the lobby. Skaters perch on them, lacing up their boots and talking. A few look up at us, and I give them a tentative smile. Mom grabs my hand and pulls me over to a knot of adults. My face flushes. Why does she have to yank me around like a little kid in front of everyone?

"Hello," Mom says to the group.

They stop talking and look at us. I wrench my hand out of Mom's grasp and cross my arms.

"You must be Laura Azarian-Carter." A tall man wearing polished black skates steps forward and thrusts his hand out.

Mom shakes it. "Yes. And this is Kaitlin, my daughter." She nudges me forward toward the group. I stumble and smile at the man.

He grins, and large dimples appear in his cheeks. Something about his smile makes me relax a little. “I’m Greg Stevenson, the skating director here. I used to star in the Skating Sensation touring show before I became a coach.”

I wonder what a circus-themed touring show has to do with anything, but Mom looks pleased. She smiles and nods.

“A great show. We took Kaitlin to see that when she was little. She loved it so much, she wanted to be in it. You wanted to be one of the dancing elephants, Kaitlin, remember?”

I look at the floor and wish I could disappear.

Greg just lets out a booming laugh and says, “Thank you, thank you.” He gestures at the two women wearing skates next to him. “This is Svetlana Priaskaya.” He puts a hand on the shoulder of the short, round woman stuffed into a fur coat. She nods at us but doesn’t smile. Instead she looks me up and down like she’s analyzing me.

I shift from foot to foot and look toward the other, younger woman with the braided hair and tie-dyed fleece jacket.

“I’m Karilee Clemmons,” she says.

Mom reaches out to shake her hand, but Karilee steps forward and grabs Mom in a hug. Mom’s arms stick out around Karilee, and her eyes are like saucers. I cover my mouth so I don’t start cracking up.

"We're so glad you're here!" Karilee says. "We love new skaters. It brings good energy to the group dynamic."

Greg checks the clock on the wall and gestures at the doors to the ice. "Why don't you put your skates on, Kaitlin? Freestyle starts in five minutes," he says as he zips up his jacket. He turns to introduce Mom to some of the other parents, and I catch the words SKATING SENSATION written across the back of his jacket in sparkling silver thread.

I put my bag in front of the nearest chair.

"Don't sit on that one. It's broken," the girl across from me says.

"Thanks." I move to the next chair. It looks like it has thirty-year-old dirt embedded in the seat. I try not to think about it as I pull my skates on.

"Are you new?" the girl asks.

I look up and recognize the Nice Screechy Violin girl from Praterville. Is she joking? I mean, how could she forget? She's gathering her short black hair into a tiny ponytail and looking like she's never seen me before. "Yeah. I used to skate at Ridgeline, but now . . . I don't." I tie a double knot in my right skate laces and reach for my left.

The girl shrugs and fishes a pair of red gloves from her skate bag. They completely clash with her pink hoodie, but she either doesn't notice or doesn't care. "I used to skate at Pound Lake, but I don't anymore either. It's much better here."

"Oh." I wonder what happened to force her to leave a club as good as Pound Lake, but there's no way I'm going to ask. I'm sure she's just saving face by saying that Fallton is better, when everyone knows otherwise.

She tilts her head. "Weren't you at Praterville?"

Now she remembers. I take a deep breath as I search for my own gloves. "Yeah."

She breaks into a smile. "I knew it! You had that really great program to *Swan Lake*, right?"

I blink at her. "Um, yeah. That was me."

"So, are you going to skate here now . . . what's your name?"

"Kaitlin," I say as I stand up and follow her out to the ice. "Maybe."

"I'm Miyu. It's Japanese." She runs the words together like she has to explain this every day.

No one is actually skating yet. All the skaters and coaches are busy stabbing and scraping at the ice with their blades. Some of them are even hacking away at it with little shovels. I try to figure out what they're doing as I cross the rink with Miyu.

She glides to the boards on the opposite side, where she deposits her skate guards and music. I put my stuff next to hers.

"What's everyone doing?" I finally ask.

"Scraping down the bumps. Come on." She moves into the middle and points with her toe pick at a smooth, shiny mountain rising from the ice.

I glance down the rink. The huge bumps are in neat soldierlike rows, stretching from one end of the ice to the other. I've never seen anything like it. I mean, Ridgeline used to get little bumps sometimes, but these things are the size of Mount Everest. "How does the ice get like this?"

"It happens in the summer mostly. My mom says it has something to do with humidity and bad insulation." Miyu chops at the offending bump with her toe pick. Ice chips fly in all directions. "If you hit one of these in a spin or even just skating backward, down you go. So we smooth them out every morning."

I go to the next mountain in line and imitate Miyu by stabbing it with my blade. "How come the Zamboni doesn't fix these?"

Miyu shrugs. "The thing's been here since the dinosaurs. We're lucky it smooths the ice at all."

I chop away at my bump until it's even with the ice around it.

Once the bumps are gone, the session really begins. Most

of the skaters move around the perimeter of the ice, doing various patterns of edges and turns to warm up. But one older girl glides into center ice in front of us, turns backward, and then leaps into the air to turn three times before landing.

My eyes want to pop out of my head. Who does a triple salchow to warm up? Except maybe Michelle Kwan? The girl launches into a series of triple jumps, one right after the other. I squint to see if I can figure out who she is. She definitely looks good enough to have gone to Nationals. All I can see is that she has dark, curly hair. Wait . . .

I turn to Miyu. "Is that—"

"Jessa Hernandez. She won Nationals a couple of years ago."

"Wow." I watch Jessa dig her toe pick into the ice behind her and launch into a triple flip. She rotates three times in the air before landing gracefully on one foot. "I thought she retired after her big meltdown at Worlds. I didn't know she was skating here."

"She's been trying to make a comeback," Miyu says. "I think this is her year."

Miyu skates off to have a lesson with Karilee, the hugging coach, and I wrench my eyes from Jessa and begin to move around the rink.

As I watch Miyu work on spins, I realize how different she is from Ellery. She never mentioned my outburst at Praterville, even though she was the one who helped pick up all the medals. A smile creeps across my face as I realize *no one* here—not even the coaches—said anything about the competition. It's like it doesn't even matter to them.

I feel lighter somehow, as if the whole thing was just a bad dream. I push off and warm up with an energy I haven't felt since before Praterville. I don't think about the judges' scores or what I said. Instead I fly across the ice, taking care not to get in anyone's way. I do my favorite old crossover and turn patterns. I don't think I've ever skated this fast in my life.

It feels good.

The session flies by. With only five minutes left, I do one last double axel, my hardest jump. Skating forward on one foot, I leap up, twist around two and a half times, and land backward. Perfect. I glide to the boards, where I left my water next to Miyu's stuff. I grasp my purple plastic bottle and chug. The water's freezing cold from sitting in the rink. I can almost feel it rolling down into my stomach.

"I saw your double axel," a voice says over my shoulder. "It's pretty good."

I almost choke on the water as I spin around. A guy stands

at the boards next to me. And not just any guy. A really, really cute one.

"Um . . ." He points at my chin.

Too late, I feel the water dribbling down from my mouth and threatening to drip from my chin. I swipe at it and wish I could think of something funny to say to make him laugh.

"I'm new here," I say instead. Which is probably the dumbest thing ever.

But instead of saying *I know* or *Duh, that's obvious*, the cute guy grins. He pushes his swishy brown hair out of his eyes.

"You probably already know that," I say for him. I seriously wish I could start this whole conversation over.

"So, what's your story?" he asks as he leans against the boards. He's a little taller than me, but looks about the same age.

"My story?"

Miyu slides to a stop next to me. "This is Kaitlin," she says to him. "She's checking us out to see if we're good enough for her."

"No, that's not—" I start to say, but Swishy Hair nods.

"She's gotta have a story, or why else would she be here?" he says.

Miyu taps her blade guards against her gloved hand and narrows her eyes at him. "Don't you have something to practice?"

He ignores Miyu and waves at me. "See you Monday, Double Axel. Tell me your story then."

"What was he talking about?" I ask Miyu when he leaves.

She shakes her head. "Who knows?"

Swishy Hair swoops by us and jumps into a perfect double axel.

And I realize I'm looking forward to seeing him again Monday.

Chapter Six

DUH. THAT'S Y IT'S FALL DOWN CLUB.

I read the text from Ellery and try to think of what to say next. Houses and stores slip by the van window as the sun starts to come up. It's Monday morning, and I can imagine Ellery texting as her mom drives her to Ridgeline.

Mom was so excited about me officially joining Fallton, she gave my phone back last night. The first thing I did was text Ellery about the club. She just got back to me.

My phone beeps before I get the chance to respond.

CAN'T BELIEVE UR SKATING W/ THOSE FREAKS.

NOT SO BAD, RLY, I type.

WHATEVER.

C U SOON.

I wait for a response. When nothing comes, I stuff the phone into my skate bag. I just wish she was happy I'm skating again, the way Dad was when I told him Fallton didn't seem so bad. After all, Miyu was really nice. Jessa Hernandez skates there, and then there was that guy with the perfect hair who called me Double Axel. And even though none of the coaches are Hildy, Greg seemed really into working with me and didn't even mention my fiasco at Praterville.

Best of all, I'd be unstoppable at Regionals if I could skate with that wonderful, light feeling like I had on Saturday. That feeling I used to have moving around the rink at Ridgeline, where nothing exists except me and the ice. If I work hard, maybe I can make the judges forget what happened at Praterville—and those embarrassing apology letters Mom made me write—and be back on track to qualifying for Nationals.

In the rink lobby, I find an empty chair—one that's not broken—and pull out my skates. Miyu is talking with some other skaters. She waves. I wave back. I'm wondering if I should join her when Mom sits next to me.

She consults a sheet of paper from her purse. "I signed you up for two free skate sessions this morning. You have a lesson with Greg first thing. They don't have skating again until later this afternoon, so we'll go home and you can do your schoolwork. Then when we come back, you have a couple more practice sessions and an off-ice class. Oh, and we'll have to join a gym, since there's no exercise equipment here. You can't slack off on your strength training."

I yawn just thinking about it all. As I lace up my skates, I watch through the rink windows as a slender blond woman makes camp on the bleachers. She lays out a blanket, pours coffee into a mug from a thermos, and pulls a notebook and pen from a huge orange bag. She has to be someone's mom, although I don't know why she's sitting out in the cold by herself when she could watch just fine from the lobby with most of the other parents.

"Kaitlin! It's so nice to see you. Are you ready to work?" Greg looms over me, smiling as if seeing me is the best thing that's ever happened to him.

I double-knot my laces and stand. "Ready."

"Skate hard!" Mom shouts after us. She's already moving toward her usual rink activity—gossiping with the other parents. I swear Mom knows more about skating than I do, and she's never even been on the ice.

I pull my guards off and glide toward the far wall to

deposit my stuff before working on the ice bumps. As I dig into the nearest one, someone flies past me. The girl is blond, about my age, and wearing this expensive practice dress Ellery and I drooled over when we saw it at a designer's booth at the last competition.

"Addison! Time to kill the bumps," Greg yells at her.

She comes to a graceful stop next to us and daintily jabs her toe pick at an extra-large bump while she glares at me. "Who are you?"

I stare at her for a moment. Everyone was so nice on Saturday. Who in the world is this girl? "Kaitlin." I give her a smile.

Addison doesn't smile back.

"Kaitlin, why don't you start down near the Zamboni garage?" Greg winks.

I skate off to the end of the ice—far away from Addison. One by one, the other skaters trickle out, and the bumps are gone in no time. Greg gives me ten minutes to warm up before my lesson, and I take off across the rink with the same free feeling I had on Saturday.

It's not until I start my jumps that I notice Addison again.

She's doing the exact same jumps, right after I land them. I do an axel, she does an axel. I squeak out the landing of a double flip–double toe loop combination—two jumps, one right after the other—and she does the same thing perfectly.

The little hairs on my arms rise. It feels like she's following me, copying me. As if we're in a competition and she's trying to show judges—or maybe just me—that she can do everything better.

I don't have anything to prove to her. I know I'm a good skater, never mind what the last judges thought. I push across the rink and move on to spins. I lower myself into a back sit spin, rotating on my right leg with my left leg extended in front and my rear end just inches from the ice. Addison does the exact same thing. I'm spinning so fast that everything's a little blurry, but it looks like she just twisted her body into a pretzel-like position I've never seen before.

How did she do that? I whip my head around so I can see her again, forgetting that it will slow my spin. I lose the careful balance on my blade and it shoots out from underneath me, leaving me spinning on my behind.

Addison pulls up from her twisted sitting position and finishes with a fast upright spin. She glides over to me and smirks. "Nice butt spin."

I open my mouth to say something back, but then I shut it. It's only my second day here. I can't be rude to people, even if they're rude to me. I search for something nice to say.

"Thanks. I've been working on it," is all I can come up with. It sounds like one of Dad's jokes.

She doesn't laugh. Instead she squats next to me. Her hairline shows brown roots, and I try not to stare at it. Her mom lets her dye her hair? Mine won't even let me wear makeup unless I'm performing.

She narrows her brown eyes. "Your double toe was under-rotated. You don't turn fast enough after you take off. That's why you could barely land it."

My face burns. Who does this girl think she is? A coach? I scramble to get up from the ice. She rises gracefully and looks me in the eye.

"You won't ever get past Juvenile with an under-rotated double toe."

I clench my gloved hands into fists at my sides. How does she even know what level I'm on? I don't remember seeing her at competitions. I wish she would just go away.

And she does. With one last smirk, she turns and pushes off across the rink. I glance around, sure I have an audience. But, just as before, everyone is busy with their own practices.

Greg calls my name. I force myself to take a couple of deep breaths as I move my feet to start my lesson.

I show Greg my arsenal of jumps and spins. I try a few triple salchows and fall on each one.

He reaches out a hand to help me up after the third one. "That's a good start. This is a jump you have to master, though, if you want to move on. Triple sal was the minimum required jump to be cast in the Skating Sensation."

Since the Skating Sensation doesn't even exist anymore, I don't think I'll be trying out for it anytime soon. "I've only been working on it for a couple of months," I say.

"You don't need it until next year, so you've got time. Did you bring your music? I want to see your program."

I grab my CD and give it to the ice monitor. As I glide toward center ice, my throat goes dry. I want Greg to see me as the girl who could win Regionals, the one who's got Olympic potential. Not the girl who almost placed last at Praterville. Mom's always saying first impressions are the most important, and I want Greg to have the right first impression of me. Skating my full program—perfectly—is a chance to show him what I've got.

I arch my arms over my head and lean slightly to the right. Addison's watching me even as she runs through some footwork. I close my eyes for a second. *Focus. Stop thinking about her and just skate.* The first notes of the music sound over the speakers, and I move my arms out and down.

I follow the movement of my left hand with my eyes and see something weird.

My hand is shaking.

"No one is watching," I whisper to myself. As I take my first steps, I clench and unclench my hands to make them behave. I know this program. There's no reason for me to be nervous at all. I need to think about what I'm doing—one thing at a time.

Stroke, turn, arms out. Spiral. I stretch my right leg out behind me as high as it will go. I arch my back until I feel the muscles pulling, and hold that position for five counts.

Hildy put the double flip at the very beginning of the program. Turn backward. Reach back with right arm. Extend right foot behind me. Toe into ice. Vault into air and pull arms in hard. The two rotations happen almost too fast to count. I land solidly on my right foot. A smile covers my face as I thrust my arms out and stretch my left leg behind me.

The music continues, and I think my way through the jumps and spins and steps of the program. I turn and set up the hardest jump in the program—the double axel. No one else at Praterville even tried one. I glide backward on my right foot, ready to step forward and launch myself into the air, when someone shouts.

"Watch out!"

Chapter Seven

I rise up on my toe pick and screech to a stop.

Addison's right behind me. Adrenaline rushes through my body as I realize what might've just happened.

"Oops, sorry," she says in a sickly-sweet voice as I maneuver around her and try to catch up to my music.

My heart is thumping overtime and my legs feel like spaghetti, but I push on. One thing at a time. Double lutz. It's just like a double flip, except I'm gliding into the jump on the outside edge of my blade instead of the inside edge. That tiny little change of edge makes all the difference. I pick my other toe into the ice and start to turn hard into the air. My body leans off to the side as I rotate. I land—just barely—but don't have nearly enough speed or balance for the double loop that comes right after. I try it anyway, pulling my legs together as I twist up and off my right foot. My blade hits the ice too early, and I fall hard on my side.

I scramble up and hear giggling over the music. Addison stands not five feet away at the entrance to the ice, smiling with the blond woman who's been sitting on the bleachers through the whole session. They look so much alike, the woman has to be Addison's mother.

I force myself back into the program. My hands are shaking again, and it takes all my willpower to finish. As the last notes of *Swan Lake* fade, I arch my arms over my head in the same pose I started with.

Breathing hard, I grab my water bottle from the boards where Greg is waiting. I gulp the freezing water as I wait for his judgment. It really wasn't bad—except for the missed double axel and the fall. And he had to see how Addison messed those up.

Greg shoves his hands into the pockets of his jacket. He's looking across the ice. I turn my head to see who he's watching, but there's no one in his line of vision.

"How do you feel about that program?" he asks out of nowhere.

I take a deep breath. "I missed the double axel. I know I messed up the combination jump, but my timing was off," I say as fast as possible. Greg's quiet, so I add, "I think I rushed the flying camel, too." I'd jumped too fast from one foot to the other to start the flying camel, so when I stretched my left leg out behind me in the spin, I wobbled a little bit. But only for a second. The rest of the spin was fine.

"The jumps and spins were good. But I'm not talking about that particular run-through. The program as a whole—do you like it?" Greg turns his head to study me.

What does he mean, do I like it? "I suppose so." I'm not sure if that's the right answer.

"Do you feel connected to it, like you're leaving a piece of yourself on the ice when you skate it?" Greg's eyes burrow into mine, as if he's trying to see into my soul.

I cast my gaze down and pull on the fingers of my black-and-purple-striped glove. "Um . . . I guess? I love skating." It feels like he's giving me a test I haven't studied for. Hildy never asked stuff like this. Her questions were more like, "Did you count the revolutions in that camel spin?" and "Why didn't you do the bit of choreography before the footwork?" Things I knew the answers to.

"I guess?" Greg repeats.

I shrug and sneak a look at the clock on the hockey scoreboard. It's 5:57. Only three minutes left in this session. I can't get away from Greg and his weird questions fast enough. Mom's right about first impressions. I obviously blew this one.

"Kaitlin," Greg says.

I snap my eyes back to him.

"You'll never skate a memorable, winning program until you put your whole self into it. Not just physically, but emotionally. You need to feel something in order to make the judges and the audience fall in love with you. Your personality has to shine through."

I blink at him. The program has expressive choreography. What about that part at the beginning where I'm arched sideways? And the footwork, where I point my toes and make balletic movements with my arms?

"Showing personality and emotion is more than just waving your arms around and imitating movements someone else has come up with," Greg says as if he read my mind. "What was your program components score at Praterville?"

"Nine point six five," I whisper. My throat is prickling.

"Hmm." Greg rubs his chin with his hand. "Seems like the judges agreed with me. I haven't seen your protocols, but

I'm guessing they docked you on interpretation, choreography, and performance."

That's exactly what the score sheet said. I only stared at it for hours last week, trying to figure out what went so wrong. I bite my lip. The prickling intensifies, and my eyes get watery. I can't cry in front of Greg. I can't, I can't, I can't.

"Session's over," the ice monitor calls from the entrance. A few skaters, the ones not staying for the second morning session, move toward the ice entrance.

"I think I know just what you need." Greg thumps his mittened hand against the top of the boards. "I'll bring it this afternoon."

Addison skids to a stop a foot away, spraying ice all over me. I look down at my snow-covered pants and resist the urge to wipe them dry.

"Isn't it time for my lesson?" she asks Greg without even looking at me.

"It is," Greg says. "See you this afternoon, Kaitlin. And remember, you can't be a star without twinkling." He leads Addison out toward center ice.

I stare after him. What does that mean? And, more importantly, does he really think I'm as boring as the Praterville judges thought? It's like he didn't even see how difficult my program is. Didn't notice how Hildy chose every single element to show off my soaring jumps and fast spins. My eyes prick again, and I squeeze them shut. I can't think about that now, or I'll start crying in front of everyone.

I go through the motions of practice for the next hour, but my mind is on whatever it is Greg's bringing this afternoon.

At least it is until Swishy Hair comes to a stop next to me while I'm sipping water at the boards. I didn't realize how tall he was yesterday. Now he's towering over me, although he doesn't look like he's very much older.

"I saw what happened with your program," he says. "Don't worry about Addison. She's just really competitive, especially with those at her level. We tune her out."

"Oh. So . . . everyone just puts up with her?"

"And her mom."

I'm dying to ask why. I mean, the fact that I got kicked out of my old club for saying what I thought to the judges and accidentally knocking over a bunch of medals—but Addison doesn't for being awful all the time—hardly seems fair.

"You're dying to know why, right?"

I shake my head, but he just laughs.

"Yes, you are. It's in your eyes."

I look away from him, like I'm suddenly really interested

in watching everyone else skate. How can he read my eyes, anyway? They're just eyes.

"Come on, admit it, Double Axel," he says.

I watch a pair of ice dancers maneuver around the rink. The guy flips the girl into a crazy lift. Her head is just inches from the ice. Just as I'm sure she's going to slip from his grasp and hit her head, he grabs her waist and pulls her into a standing position. Then they separate and move into some strange dance, flailing their arms over their heads and leaning forward. It doesn't look like any ice dance I've ever seen.

I take a deep breath and turn back toward Swishy Hair. "Okay, fine. Why is Addison allowed to skate here if she's so awful?"

"Why are you here?" he asks in return.

"I was kind of kicked out of my old club."

"Everyone here has a story." He sweeps his arm around, taking in everyone on the ice. "Look around."

I do, but all I see are people skating. "What do you mean?"

But he's already gone. I spot him headed toward Jessa Hernandez, who's also taking a water break on the other side of the rink. Jessa, the National champion who completely lost it at Worlds two years ago and could barely land a single jump in her free program. Everyone thought for sure she'd given up when she didn't even show for Nationals the next year.

Nearby, Karilee's hugging one of her students.

Wait. The ice dancers with the crazy moves. Jessa, the meltdown queen. Mean Addison and her over-the-top stage mom. Miyu, who's super nice, not super good, and who left Pound Lake for some mysterious reason. Karilee, the touchy-feely coach. Greg, who seems just a little hung up on his former ice show. The Russian coach who stared me down.

Everyone here is just a little bit . . . weird. Was Ellery right? Am I weird too? Or maybe I'm just stuck here, like the Swishy Hair guy, who couldn't be weird if he tried.

And what's his story?

Chapter Eight

I've spent the day staring down the clock and dreading Greg's big surprise. At Ridgeline, I would've hung around at the rink all day, doing schoolwork on my laptop between practice sessions and having lunch at the lobby café. But since hardly anyone homeschools at Fallton, and there isn't any skating in the middle of the day, Mom and I went home after the morning sessions.

But I couldn't stop thinking about what Greg has planned. I had to read my chapter for science three times because I couldn't pay attention. And I'm pretty sure the personal trainer at my new gym thinks I'm a flake, since I kept zoning out during reps on the leg-lift machine.

Mom's positive Greg's just going to record me or make me skate with a hockey stick in both hands for better posture. I'm not so sure. Those seem really tame for Mr. Skating Sensation.

So now I'm back at the rink, and about to find out. After the off-ice Movement and Interpretation class, anyway.

Mom gives me a nudge toward the far end of the lobby. "The class is about ready to start. At least it'll take your mind off your lesson."

Somehow I doubt it.

Everyone's gathered in a bunch, talking and waiting for the class to begin. I find a spot between Miyu and Jessa. And try not to get all starstruck over the fact that I'm standing right next to Jessa Hernandez.

"What do you think Greg's surprise is?" I ask Miyu. I told her about it before we left this morning.

"Probably some whacked-out costume from his ice show days. He'll make you put it on and act out the character," she says as she bends down to retie one of her shoes.

"No way. Are you serious? I'd die of embarrassment." I still can't get over how easy it is to talk to Miyu. Even though we just met, I can say things to her I never would've said to Ellery.

Miyu flashes me a smile. "You're making me glad I have Karilee as a coach instead of Greg."

"Maybe it's just a video camera, so I can see . . . whatever it is he sees."

"I vote for the crazy costume. Maybe you'll have to be a monkey. Or a clown. Ooh! Or an elephant!" Miyu cracks up.

I force a laugh. The idea is funny, as long as it doesn't actually happen. There's no way I'll skate at my new rink in front of everyone dressed as an elephant. I'd never live it down.

Karilee wafts into the group. She doesn't look anything like a skating coach right now. Instead of the tie-dyed jacket, she's wearing a long, flowy skirt and flower-printed top. Her long hair hangs loose around her face. I can't believe she's going to show us off-ice exercises in that outfit. Mom's eyes are probably bugging out of her head from across the lobby. I look around to see if anyone else is confused. They're all looking straight ahead at Karilee, even Jessa. I guess this is normal for Karilee.

"Good afternoon, everyone," she says in a singsong voice that reminds me of my kindergarten teacher. "Today we're going to focus on rhythm and flow and music. Something a little different." She reaches down and hits a button on the CD player. Some kind of weird, chanting music—like monks in a church—erupts from the speakers.

"Everyone please take a seat." Karilee sinks to the rubber-matted floor and tucks her feet underneath her. The long skirt billows out and slowly drifts down.

I eye the floor. It's covered in grit and damp in places from melted ice. Miyu's already sitting, despite the unidentified dirt. I sneak a glance at Jessa. She wrinkles her face a little, takes a deep breath, and sits.

I do the same, trying not to think of the shiny, wooden-floored room with yoga mats at my old rink. Do Olympic champions learn stretching exercises on dirty rink floors?

"Forgot to bring my towel," Jessa whispers.

It takes me a second to realize she's talking to me. "Me too," I finally say. I look around and realize everyone else—except Miyu and Karilee—is sitting on a towel or a mat.

"Listen to the music," Karilee says. "Then do what feels natural—just with your upper body." She closes her eyes, and then begins to sway back and forth. She raises her arms over her head and waves them in time to the chanting. She looks absolutely insane.

A giggle rises in my throat, and I cough to cover it up. Jessa's not so lucky. She laughs, and a few others join her. Not Miyu, though. She's totally into it, rocking from side to side with her eyes closed.

Karilee's eyes fly open. "Yes, we may look funny. But how do you expect to figure out what looks good unless you're willing to risk looking silly? I want to see *everyone* moving to the music. Close your eyes if you feel self-conscious."

I shut my eyes and move back and forth like Miyu. I raise my arms at the elbows and wave my hands. At least Swishy Hair isn't here to see me look like this.

"Extend your arms. Reach out as far as you can, then reach even farther. Stretch out your fingertips."

I do what she says and remind myself that everyone else is doing the same thing. We all look stupid together. And—hopefully—we all have our eyes closed.

"Move your arms back and forth. Find your rhythm."

I move my arms farther to the side. "Sorry," Miyu and I whisper to each other when our hands smack together.

"Now try forward and back. Lean down to the floor. Then arch backward, as far as you can go."

I reach forward, my nose inches from the disgusting rubber mats. As the smell of feet and dirty water enters my nostrils, I move back up. And try not to think of how many hockey players have spit on the floor.

"Now arch your back. Tummy to the ceiling!"

I bend back as far as I can.

And fall over.

But I don't just land on the gritty, damp floor. My arms, stretched over my head, connect with a pair of standing legs. I didn't think anyone was behind me. My eyes pop open.

A face tilts down and grins at me. It's Swishy Hair.

"Hey, there, Double Axel. I know you missed me, but you don't have to hug my legs," he says.

I jerk back into a sitting position. Everyone has their eyes open now, even Karilee. My face goes warm, and I wish we could just get back to waving our arms with our eyes closed.

"How nice of you to join us, Mr. Walker," Karilee says. "Ten minutes late, as usual."

"Sorry," he says offhandedly. He plops himself onto the floor on the other side of Miyu, no towel or mat, and stretches out his long legs. His hair falls into his face, but he doesn't bother pushing it out of the way.

Miyu turns to me and rolls her eyes. I kind of wish he'd been able to sit next to me, even though I'm totally mortified at having accidentally grabbed his legs.

"All right, let's stand up. Now we're going to do full-body movement. Try walking or jumping or doing whatever you feel interprets the music. Don't forget to use your arms." Karilee stands on one foot like a flamingo and waves her arms again. The class slowly moves into action. Some people are really into it, like Miyu, who's taking giant steps in a circle with her arms raised straight overhead, while others—like me—are waiting to see what everyone else does.

"Let's just spin in circles until we get dizzy and fall down," Swishy Hair says in my ear.

"Um . . ." I don't know if this is a good idea.

"Or, better yet, let's chicken dance. C'mon, Kaitlin, chicken dance with me!" He tucks his hands under his arm-pits and starts flapping his elbows like a chicken. He bobs his head in rhythm with the chanting, and his hair hides his eyes.

I look around. Miyu's staring up at her arms and is in her own world. The ice dancer guy I saw this morning is doing some crazy interpretive dance in the corner by the gumball machine.

"Are you too chicken to be a chicken?" Swishy Hair flaps an elbow wing against my shoulder.

No one's watching, so what does it matter? Even Mom's busy chatting with the other parents. And this is all about musical interpretation, right?

"Okay," I finally say.

"Let's go, then." He bobs his head and struts around the group, elbows flapping. I tuck up my hands and follow him.

We weave between Addison and a short brown-haired girl. Addison eyes me, her eyebrows raised as she swings her arms from side to side. I bite my lip, and my arms droop a little.

Swishy Hair looks back. "Really, Double Axel, is that all you've got?"

I wish I could feel as free as he does. Everyone looks stupid—moving their arms all over and stomping around our little corner of the lobby.

Just go for it, Kaitlin, I order myself. *No one cares.* I take a deep breath and flap my arms harder. I lift my knees, mimicking the cute guy.

We tromp around the group. It really isn't so bad. In fact, it's kind of fun.

"Fly, chicken, fly!" he calls back to me.

I flap my arms harder and slide between two girls pretending to be trees. My right elbow collides with something hard.

"Ow!" someone yells behind me.

I drop my arms and spin around. Addison's standing right there, clutching her nose.

Chapter Nine

"What's your problem?" Addison squeals in a nasal voice.

"Oh my God, I'm sorry! Are you okay?" I reach toward her, but she backs away from me.

"Girls, what's going on?" Karilee floats toward us. "Addison, are you all right?"

Addison winces. "The new girl broke my nose."

"I—I didn't mean to." Did I really hit her hard enough to break her nose?

"Let me see." Karilee pulls Addison's hand away from her face.

"I'll bleed all over the place!"

"Honey, there's no blood." Karilee gently touches Addison's nose. "I don't think anything's broken. It'll just be sore for a while."

"What happened? Addison?" Addison's mother pushes aside the crowd that's gathered around us.

"She got bumped in the nose. She'll be okay with some ice," Karilee says.

Addison's mom peers into her daughter's face. "I don't know. We're going to the urgent care center."

"Kaitlin did it," Addison says with a breaking voice. She points at me.

"I'm really sorry." I want to shrink back into the other skaters.

"It was an accident," Karilee says.

Addison's mom glares at me. "You need to be more careful."

I can't help but think of this morning, when Addison nearly plowed me over while I was in my program. But I don't say anything. I just swallow hard.

Karilee claps. "I think we're finished for today. Everyone get ready for the session. And remember to take what you've learned here and apply it to your programs."

Skaters disperse across the lobby as Addison's mom pulls her toward the hallway and the door. Swishy Hair winks at me like nothing awful just happened. He sits on a nearby chair and puts on his skates.

Miyu grabs my arm. "Watch out for Braedon. He's nothing but trouble."

"Who's Braedon?" I ask Miyu as I follow her to the chairs.

She frowns at me. "That guy you were following around and being stupid with."

So that's his name. Braedon Walker. "But he seems really nice."

"Charming," she corrects me. "But a total—"

"Kaitlin, what happened?" Mom jumps in before Miyu can finish her sentence. "Here, put your skates on and tell me."

"I just bumped into someone. It's no big deal," I say as I shove my right foot into my skate. The last thing I need is Mom freaking out about Addison and her mom's reaction. I'm glad Miyu left her skates on the other side of the lobby, although somehow I know she wouldn't give away the truth.

"But I saw Addison and Mrs. Thomas leave, and they didn't look happy."

"They're just going to get ice and then she'll be back." I concentrate on lacing my boot tightly so I don't have to look at Mom.

"They could've gotten ice here at the snack bar."

I shrug. "Maybe they decided to go home so Addison could take it easy."

"Her mother is a strange one," Mom says. "She doesn't seem to talk to any of the other parents. She just watches Addison all the time and writes in that notebook. Like a skating stage mom."

Like you, I think. But that's something I definitely don't say out loud. At least Mom doesn't watch every move I make on the ice.

"Come on, I think Greg's waiting for you. Now, whatever the surprise is, just go along with it. We're lucky he wants to coach you at all. You can't lose this opportunity," Mom says.

I'd been breathing a little easier until Mom said that. Visions of an elephant costume dance in my head.

Greg's standing at the ice entrance, drinking a cup of coffee. I pull off my guards and wait for him to say something.

All he says is, "Go warm up."

I drop my stuff on the boards and fly through my warm-up, crossing over one foot, barely holding the position, and then crossing over the other. I've spent all day worrying about this moment, but now that it's here, I just want to get it over with. I skid to a stop in front of him, completely out of breath.

"I've never seen anyone do Russian stroking that fast," he says with a grin. "Not even Helmut Pryor."

"Who?"

"The star of Skating Sensation when I first joined."

"Oh." I'm only halfway paying attention. I glance at the bleachers behind Greg. There's no sign of any horrible costume. At least I won't have to prance around the rink like Giggles the Clown or something.

"All right. Follow me." Greg moves off toward the lobby.

I throw on my guards and follow him, hurrying to keep up. What if he's hidden the costume in the coaches' room, or outside in his car? I cross my fingers.

We bang through the doors. Mom spots us and raises her eyebrows. I shrug and follow Greg to the coaches' room. He pushes the door open and begins rustling through a duffel bag on one of the benches. I peer in from the doorway, crossing my fingers so hard they start to tingle.

Greg pulls a CD from the bag and pops it into Karilee's boom box. He motions at me to come in. I hesitate for a second before sliding in to stand next to the door. Skaters weren't allowed in the coaches' room at my old rink. Everyone joked that the coaches had a big-screen TV and a chocolate fountain, and that's why they didn't want skaters coming in. There's nothing like that here—just a big, mostly empty room with concrete-block walls and a few benches with peeling paint.

Some kind of dramatic violin music streams from the speakers. Greg taps his fingers on the top of the boom box in time to the music. When it's finished, another piece starts. This one sounds like an orchestra with an electric guitar. Almost like the guitarist from a rock band got lost and ended up in the middle of the woodwind section. That piece ends, and a third one with a lot of drums starts. I shift from foot to foot. Why are we hanging around listening to music?

The third piece ends, and Greg looks at me. "Do you like any of those?"

"Sure, I guess."

"Which one do you like best?"

"Um . . ." This is the weirdest thing ever. I'm not sure why he cares which piece was my favorite.

Greg pops the CD out of the boom box. "Which one speaks to you?"

"The first one, I guess?" That one was kind of sassy and powerful. I liked it. In fact, I kind of want him to burn me a copy of it. It would be perfect to add to my collection of workout music.

“Great choice,” Greg replies. “A tango. It’s . . .” He snaps his fingers as he searches for the right word. “Diva music. So that’s your new program piece.”

My heart falls into my stomach.

“My new . . . what?” I squeak out.

Chapter Ten

"Program," he repeats. "You need something that exudes personality. That connects with the audience. And that makes the judges sit up and take notice."

"Okay," is all I can say. Inside, my brain is screaming. It's too late to change my program. What was wrong with *Swan Lake*? It's soft and pretty. Everything this music isn't. Ellery could skate a tango. Addison could definitely do a tango. But me? Hildy always called my style light and balletic.

Not to mention that I'm pretty sure the judges have already taken notice of me. And not in a good way.

"A tango." I say the words like they're some foreign language.

"That was your favorite, right?"

I nod. It was . . . just not for my program.

"Then let's start choreographing it. With enough hard work, it should be polished and ready to go for Regionals."

"Wait," I say as Greg leaves the coaches' room. "I . . ." Mom's words echo through my head. I can't mess up this opportunity. It's the only one I have. "Um . . . never mind."

Numb, I follow Greg back to the ice. He hands the CD to the ice monitor.

Maybe it won't be so bad. Once he sees how much tango doesn't suit me, he'll change his mind and go back to *Swan Lake*. Or he'll just give up on me.

Wait. What if he does give up? Then where will I skate? We'll have to move across the country to find a new coach. Or I'll have to quit and kiss my Olympic dream good-bye. I'll have to take up hockey or softball or some sport where they'll accept my loud mouth and lack of tango ability.

"Let's tango!" Greg says as he hops onto the ice.

"Okay." I try to say it with enthusiasm.

Strains of the dramatic music fill the rink. I trail after Greg as he walks through the program. "We'll keep all of the same jumps and spins as your old program but move them around to fit this music," he calls over his shoulder as he demonstrates where everything will go. "Now this will be the footwork sequence. We'll fill it in later with something flirty. Then stroke, stroke, layback spin combination with your arms like this." Greg puts his hands on his hips.

I follow him without saying anything.

"Then some fun little steps here." Greg flies through a series of turns and hops diagonally across the ice. "And we need something before you do the first combination jump. What do you think?"

What do I what?

"Is there something you'd like to do before the jumps?" He skids to a stop and waits for an answer.

This is so not at all what I'm used to. Hildy always had my programs choreographed before she showed them to me, usually with the help of a professional choreographer. If something didn't work, she'd change it, but she definitely never asked *me* what I wanted to do.

"Come on, Kaitlin. There's got to be something you'd love to have in this program," Greg says.

"A spread eagle," I say right away. I love gliding along on a deep edge with my feet turned out, heel to heel.

He smiles. "Perfect. It fits the music. And it'll make doing the jumps right after a lot harder, which will give you a better score—if you can do it."

"I can do it." Hildy never put a spread eagle in any of my programs, and I'm not about to let Greg change his mind now that he's agreed to it.

"Now, what about after this double lutz–double loop combo? You need to start another spin right on this change in the music, but we have a few seconds to fill right before that."

And he does that for the rest of the program. I get to add in all the moves I love—a Biellmann spiral, where I grab my foot from behind and pull it up over my head, a split jump, and all kinds of other things I never got to do in a program before.

It's actually kind of fun, until I remember that I'm supposed to do this program perfectly in less than two months at Regionals.

"Last jump is double axel. Then finish with a kicky little stag jump and a show stop." He does the show stop, turning his right foot out and placing it in front of his left foot so the blade skids to a halt.

I'm out of breath even though I haven't even been doing anything. My hardest jump, at the very end of the program, when I have no energy left and my legs feel like mush?

"It's not an easy program," Greg says. "It's challenging,

but I know you can do it. Let's show those judges you deserve a second chance."

I nod. But inside, I'm completely freaking out.

We spend the rest of the lesson nailing down the program in pieces. By the end, I have it memorized, even though I don't know whether I can actually do the whole thing. And do it with what Greg calls "personality."

When the lesson is finally over, Greg talks to Mom about my program. I cross my fingers and hope she'll insist on *Swan Lake.* And what Mom wants, she always gets. Maybe Greg will let me add a spread eagle to it.

"A tango! How daring. I love it," she says when Greg tells her. "And you think it'll be ready by Regionals?"

What? *No!* No, no, no, no, no.

Mom and Greg keep talking around me.

"If Kaitlin works at it," Greg says. "She's an extremely talented skater, but the judges will never see that unless she really engages them. She needs to come out of her shell."

I bite my lip to keep all the nos from falling out. I'm standing right here, and he's talking about me like I'm invisible.

"I'm thinking we'll have to add some ice dance lessons too. We're going to turn you into a skater the judges can't possibly look away from." Greg squeezes my shoulder as he heads back to the ice.

They won't be able to look away from me because I'll be the only girl who can't get through her program. This is what I get for joining the Fall Down Club.

I have to say something. I can't let my dream die without a fight.

I look from Mom to Greg, who's almost to the rink doors. I have a better chance with him than with her. "I just have to ask Greg something," I say to Mom before I run after Greg.

"Wait!" I stumble over my blade guards into the doors.

"Kaitlin? You okay?" Greg grabs my arm, and I manage not to fall in an ungraceful heap on the floor.

"Sorry, I'm fine. I just . . ." How am I going to say this without completely offending him? "I'm not sure about the new music. I mean, it's really fun and intense and I like it, but I don't know if it's me. I don't know if I can skate it the way you think I can."

I cross my fingers behind my back and hope he doesn't dump me the way Hildy did. He smiles just a little as we step out of the way to let Svetlana and the crazy ice dance team move through the doors. Smiling can't be bad, right? Maybe he agrees with me.

"Do you trust me?" he asks.

"Um . . . yes." At least, that sounds like a question I should say yes to. I barely even know him, but I don't think he'd want to sabotage my skating career. He wouldn't be much of a coach if he did that.

"Then trust me on this. You need fiery music. And believe me, you can skate it—but only if you let yourself."

"But that's it. I don't think I can. My style is softer, lighter. Not . . . fiery."

"Then who was that girl who told the judges exactly how she felt at Praterville?"

"*That* was an accident," I say.

"Knocking all the medals off the table was an accident. You speaking your mind wasn't. You've got a bold, fiery side that's just dying to come out."

For the nine hundredth time, I wish I could take back what happened at that competition.

Greg crosses his arms. "Okay. So here's the deal, and I'm not being mean. I'm being honest. If you want to be a champion, go to Nationals, maybe even the Olympics one day, you need to embrace that person you don't think you are. Or, you can do the same old thing, get the same old scores, and be happy with being mediocre. I'll coach you either way, but it's your decision."

I blink at him. "You mean I won't get to Nationals with *Swan Lake*?"

"That's exactly what I'm saying."

"But Hildy—"

"Is Hildy your coach?"

I swallow and shake my head.

"I know this sounds odd, but I think that by giving you such low components marks in your last competition, the judges were trying to push you. They can see you have the jumps and the spins. They know you have the makings of a champion, but you need to improve on the artistic side."

He's right—that doesn't make a lot of sense. But I get what he's really trying to say. It's tango or nothing. "Okay. I'll try it."

"You'll have to do more than try." Greg zips up his Skating Sensation jacket and moves toward the doors.

I imagine myself on the podium at Regionals. If a tango will get me there, I'll do it. Even if it means pretending to be someone I'm not. "I'll tango better than anyone. I promise."

Greg nods at me and disappears into the rink.

Now if only I can keep my promise.

Chapter Eleven

Pizza Supreme is packed on Thursday night. Mom only springs for pizza on special occasions, like me getting a crazy-hard new program. She claims it has too much sodium and saturated fat, and always makes Dad and me add a salad. Like the lettuce is going to zero out all the bad stuff from the pizza.

We're waiting for a table when I see them. Ellery and a bunch of kids I don't recognize are crammed into a booth along the side wall.

Mom notices them at the same time. "Isn't that Ellery? Why don't you go say hi, Kaitlin?" She gives me a little push in their direction.

"No, they look busy. I don't want to bug her." Ellery hasn't called or texted me in forever.

"I bet she'll be glad to see you. Go on, now." Mom gives me another push.

I look to Dad for help. He just grins at me.

I walk as slowly as I can toward the booth while pretending like I'm really interested in the dancing reality show blaring from the huge TVs hanging on the walls. Why does Mom always do this? I don't even know these people, except Ellery. Maybe I should act like I'm looking for the bathroom and then pretend to spot her.

Yep, I'm totally searching for the bathroom and not trying to avoid awkward conversation. Don't pay any attention to the girl who's eyeballing the wood-paneled wall like it's the most interesting thing ever.

Just as I reach the booth, I look toward the left and put on a surprised face as Ellery meets my eyes. I wave. She waves back and then starts chatting again with the guy sitting across from her.

No way am I stopping to talk. Especially since it seems like she wants nothing to do with me. I take a decisive step toward the imaginary bathrooms and almost walk right into a huge tray of pizzas and drinks blocking the middle of the aisle.

"Sorry, miss. Be just a minute." The waiter grabs a couple of drinks and some straws off the tray to give to the booth behind Ellery's.

Great. Now I'm stuck here next to Ellery with nothing to say. Thanks, Mom.

"So . . . um . . . how's everyone at the rink?" I finally ask.

Ellery looks up from her conversation. "Oh. They're fine. How's the Fall Down Club?" She giggles. The scrawny guy sitting across from her laughs. He probably has no idea what she's talking about.

"Good," I say. "Great, actually. I'm working on a new program that's totally different from anything I've done before."

Ellery gives me her full attention. "This close to Regionals? What was wrong with your old program?"

"It was kind of boring, don't you think? And I'm really close to landing my triple salchow." In my dreams. But of course I don't say that to Ellery.

She tilts her head. "But you just started working on it a couple of months ago."

"My new coach has this great technique he's teaching me. I'm so close to it. Of course, I'm not allowed to do it in my program, but I might test up to Intermediate." Now I'm just making stuff up. Aside from my first lesson, Greg hasn't even mentioned working on the triple sal. Or testing up.

"That sounds really hard," the dark-haired girl sitting next to Ellery says. "Can you do that, Ells?"

Ellery's shoulders tense up. "I'm working on it." Which is hilarious, because Ellery hasn't even landed her double axel yet.

"And I'm going to start ice dance, too." It's like my mouth won't stop. The words bubble up in my throat and fall out before I realize what I'm saying. It's just like Praterville.

"I didn't think you were into dance," Ellery says.

"That was before I had a partner," I lie.

"That sounds so romantic." Ellery's friend sighs.

Ellery shrugs. "Whatever. I hope he's cute, at least. I'm just sticking to what I do best. Singles."

The dark-haired girl giggles and pokes Ellery in the ribs. "I know who you'd like to dance with." She nods at the guy across the table.

Ellery flushes. "Cut it out."

I've never seen Ellery get embarrassed. Ever. It's weird, so I look away. The closest TV shows a couple twisting and twirling to some tense music. Kind of like my new program piece. "And I'm going to learn to dance."

"Yeah, you just said that." Ellery's face is back to a normal color, and she's frowning at me.

"No, actual dancing. Like that." I point to the TV, where the couple is gazing into each other's eyes as they sashay around the dance floor.

"Ooh, I'd love to learn ballroom dance!" Ellery's friend says.

Ellery doesn't say anything, so I keep talking. Which seems to be my thing tonight.

"And guess who's in all my sessions? Jessa Hernandez."

Ellery swirls a bread stick in some marinara sauce. "I thought she retired."

"She just took some time off. She's going to make a huge comeback. And she's helping me with my triple sal. Oh, we got a table. See you later!" I run off toward my parents. If I stood there any longer, I'd probably start telling Ellery I'd already qualified for the Olympic team. I can't believe I made all that stuff up. And then said it out loud!

"Are you all right, Pumpkin?" Dad asks as I slip into the booth. "Your face is bright red."

"Oh, yeah . . . I'm fine."

"How is Ellery? Is she ready for Regionals?" Mom asks.

"She's okay. I guess she's ready. I didn't talk to her much. She's with a bunch of friends from school."

"I'm surprised her mother hasn't started homeschooling her yet. I don't know how she'll find enough time to practice once school starts again."

I stab a bread stick with my fork and take a bite before Mom can say anything about it. Ellery was almost always at the rink before and after school. She didn't seem to have any problems balancing school and skating.

"Did you tell your father about your new program?" Before I can answer, Mom launches into a detailed description of my new music and how it will benefit my skating. Dad just smiles and nods. Mom's been talking nonstop about the program since Monday.

I swallow the last of the bread stick and fidget with my napkin. From a few booths down, I hear Ellery and her friends laugh. I guess that's what happens when you go to normal school. You have friends to get pizza with. And you share secrets. Then they tease you about the guy you like.

It looks . . . fun. I wish I went to school.

But that won't ever happen. I glance at the TV across from our booth. It's showing another couple in a studio lined with mirrors, where the guy is teaching the girl some dance steps.

Maybe talking to Ellery wasn't a complete waste of time after all.

"Hey, Mom," I say. "I have an idea that I think will help with my new program."

At practice the next day, I go through the program over and over and over. Learning the order of everything in a program is pretty easy. Actually doing it all—and doing it well—is the hard part. At the very end of the last afternoon session, I finally land all the jumps and push through the spins. Maybe it won't be so bad after all. In fact, maybe Greg will be so impressed when he sees it, he'll let me work on the triple salchow. Then at least something I told Ellery will be true.

Well, that and the dance lessons. Mom was so excited about the idea of me learning to dance for real in order to help my skating that she talked to Greg about it this morning. He agreed, so Mom called up a dance studio and signed me up for a class that starts tonight.

"Where are you off to?" Braedon asks as I follow Mom to the parking lot.

"I'm doing ballroom dancing. For my new program," I say.

"Like this?" He drops his skate bag and grabs my hands.

Before I can say anything, he's pulling me around in circles between parked cars.

"Kind of!" I'm laughing so hard, I can barely even breathe.

"Dah dah dah dah!" Braedon sings some made-up tune as he swings my arms back and forth.

"Kaitlin?" Mom's standing by the van, keys in hand. "We have to go. The studio is on the other side of town."

Braedon drops my hands and bows. Then he waves to Mom, scoops up his skate bag, and runs toward a white car waiting near the rink door.

A little out of breath, I climb into the passenger seat of Mom's car.

And it hits me that I was just holding hands with Braedon. I feel warm all over thinking about it.

"Who was that?" Mom asks as she starts the car.

"Braedon," I answer.

I can tell she wants to ask more questions, but she doesn't. And I'm glad, because I'm not sure if I'd know the answers.

Chapter Twelve

The dance studio is really just a storefront in a strip mall. It doesn't look like much, but I'm sure Mom read every review that exists on the Internet before choosing this place. So I'm betting it's more than just pretty good.

I stand behind a clump of women who are Mom's age, while Mom takes a spot in one of the chairs that line the far side of the room. There's only one other person in the chairs, so of course Mom sits right next to her and immediately starts talking. I'm the youngest one here, which feels a little weird. There are a couple of older teenagers, a girl who's standing right up front and talking to the instructor, and a boy in a baseball cap who looks like he'd rather be playing dolls with his little sister than be stuck here.

"Can I have everyone's attention, please?" The instructor raises her voice, and everyone quiets down. "This is the beginners' tango class. I'm Jill, and this is my studio. My partner Fernando will be helping us out tonight." She points to a tall, lean, dark-haired man propped against the mirrored wall.

"I am Fernando," he says with a Spanish accent, like Jill hadn't already told everyone his name. The women in front of me giggle, and Fernando shoots them a smile.

I turn back to Mom. She makes a walking motion with her fingers at me. I shake my head. No way am I moving up front. I'd rather learn to tango without anyone watching me. Besides, the women in front of me might get mad if I block their view of Fernando.

Jill raps her knuckles on the wall, and everyone looks back at her. "We will start with—"

The studio door opens, and in walks Addison and her mother. What in the world are they doing here? I shoot a glance at Mom, but she's just watching them with her eyebrows raised.

"Sorry I'm late," Addison says as she brushes past me to stand right in front of the giggling women.

Mrs. Thomas perches on a chair at the end of the row, far away from Mom and the other woman. She pulls out her notebook and pen and her phone.

Jill gives Addison a curt nod. "As I was saying, we will start with the tango hold." She snaps her fingers at Fernando, who oozes across the floor to meet her. "The lady places her arms like this, and the man like Fernando."

I stand on my tiptoes to see. The women in front of me giggle again, and Addison's already imitating Jill. I raise my arms and try to crook my left elbow the way Jill is.

Jill and Fernando move through the group, adjusting everyone's arms. Mine are starting to ache when Jill finally gets to me.

"No, no. Your left elbow needs to be down more. And your palm like this." She pulls on my arm until I'm practically wincing.

Okay, if I knew this was going to hurt, I wouldn't have signed up for it. This is way worse than crashing to the ice on a jump.

"All right, now we're going to partner up and work on the hold together. And since our ladies clearly outnumber our men, we'll have to take turns playing each role." Jill waits while everyone pairs off.

The women in front of me all pair with one another. The older girl snags the red-faced boy in the baseball cap.

Addison looks back at me and then says, "Can I partner with Fernando?"

Jill shakes her head. "Why don't you go with . . ." She points at me.

"Kaitlin," I fill in. Great. Tangoing with Addison.

Addison makes a face and slowly moves toward me. "No way am I being the guy."

"I think we're supposed to switch off," I say.

"Whatever. I'm going first, then." She flicks her hair over her shoulder and holds up her arms.

I try to imitate Fernando, but I really wasn't paying attention to what the guy is supposed to do.

"You're doing it wrong." Addison takes my left hand and moves it onto her back.

"Sorry."

We stand there for a minute waiting, while Jill helps the older women and Fernando demonstrates the correct hold for the boy in the baseball cap.

"So . . . um . . . why are you here?" I finally ask Addison.

"I wanted to learn how to dance. You know, for my skating."

"But your program is to *Phantom of the Opera*." And last time I checked, there's nothing tango-y about *Phantom*, but I don't say that.

Addison shrugs, which is kind of hard to do when you're standing in an awkward tango hold. "Maybe I'll do a tango program next year."

"Okay," I say. But I'm pretty sure I've figured out the real reason she's here—to make sure I'm not learning anything that'll make me a better skater than she is. Her mom probably overheard Greg talking about it, and immediately signed Addison up.

Fernando finally glides over to us. He gives us a once-over and clucks his tongue.

"No, no. Like this." He takes Addison's hands and almost lifts her off the floor as he shows me exactly how it should look.

Addison's face goes a little red as Fernando stares her down with this super-intense expression.

"Excuse me." Mrs. Thomas nudges me aside and starts clicking away with the camera on her phone.

"Mom!" Addison drops her arms and clenches her hands into fists at her sides.

"Good work, honey. You're a natural." Her mom pats her on the shoulder before she strolls back to the chairs.

Addison looks like she wants the floor to swallow her whole. Fernando moves on to the next pair, and I glance back at Mom. She's busy pecking away at her phone—and probably not the camera app. Mrs. Thomas starts writing in her notebook again.

"What's your mom always writing?" I ask Addison.

"None of your business." She crosses her arms and turns to listen to Jill, who's rapping on the wall again.

Oookay. I try to forget about Addison and pay attention to what Jill's saying about posture. The rest of the class time is spent practicing the hold while adding some steps. Everything is really quick and snappy. I can see exactly why Greg created the footwork sequence the way he did. It completely fits the whole tango mood.

"Good. Very good," Fernando says as he passes me testing out steps in front of the mirrors.

I smile at myself. Maybe I can do this tango thing after all.

Or maybe not.

"What are you doing with your arms?" Greg asks as I finish the last turn in the footwork during my lesson on Saturday morning. "You look so stiff."

"Um, it's the tango hold I learned at dance class." I twist

my hands together. I thought I was doing a good job of adding in what I'd learned to my program.

A corner of Greg's mouth tilts up, like he wants to smile. "I see. What you want to take from those classes is more of the *feel* of tango. The emotion of it," he says. "Not necessarily the actual dance. And relax your arms a little."

I thought I was getting the feel of the tango. I mean, I was trying to do the quick feet thing and the arms.

"I think a lesson with Svetlana will help you connect the dance with your skating," Greg says. "I'll schedule one with her this coming week. Good work today. I'll see you on Monday."

I glide to the boards to collect my stuff, and Braedon scrapes to a stop next to me. "Hey, what are you doing now?"

Is he asking me to hang out with him? I swallow hard and pay close attention to pulling off my gloves as we walk through the doors from the ice. "Just hanging out in the lobby until stretching class."

He pushes his hair out of his eyes, and I try not to stare. His eyes are really, really blue.

"We've got some time. Want to walk down to the convenience store? I need a Coke, but the snack bar's closed," he says.

"Sure, I guess." My heart leaps around in my chest. "Let me tell my mom."

"Not enough time, Double Axel. Besides, she looks busy. She'll never even notice." He sits on a chair and yanks his skates off.

I glance at Mom. She's deep in conversation with a couple of other parents. She didn't even see me get off the ice. I pull my skates off too and stuff my feet into my sneakers.

"C'mon, let's go." Braedon leads the way to the front door.

I jog after him, feeling like I'm sneaking out or something. As we walk quickly down the sidewalk toward the corner, I can't shake the feeling that I'm doing something wrong. I really should've talked to Mom. What if she's looking for me? She'll freak out when she can't find me, and I'll never hear the end of it. I should've at least grabbed my phone from my skate bag.

The bell over the door jingles as Braedon pushes it open. He pulls two Cokes from the shelf, and we make our way to the checkout counter.

"Hey, man!" A kid about our age with stringy blond hair is paying for a bag of chips.

A smile slides across Braedon's face. And I can't breathe. He's so cute, with those dimples that only come out when he smiles. I'd noticed how good-looking he was before, but now I'm really seeing it. His bright blue eyes. The dark brown hair that's just a little too long.

"Will? Hey, what's going on?" Braedon says to the stringy-haired guy.

"I heard you got kicked out of school last spring," Will says.

"Not kicked out, really. Just asked to leave," Braedon says with a grin.

I'm dying to ask what Braedon did to get kicked out.

"Now what? Homeschool?" Will asks.

"Nah. Mom knows I'm no good at that. I think she's lined up some private school over in East Washington. St. Benedict's or something."

"Wonder how long that'll last?" Will says with a laugh.

"Wanna place your bet?" Braedon replies. "At least I've only got one year till high school."

Just how many schools has Braedon been kicked out of? I tap him on the shoulder. "Hey, we've got to go. Class starts—"

Braedon wraps an arm around my shoulders. I freeze. No guy has ever done that before. It's uncomfortable and sweet at the same time. I can't figure out if I want him to move his arm or leave it where it is.

"Sorry. Forgot to introduce Kaitlin here. New girl at the rink." He gestures at Will. "This is my friend from school."

"Hey," Will says. "What's up with you?"

"Um . . . I skate. . . ."

Will and Braedon crack up like I just told the best joke ever.

"What's so funny?"

Braedon just smiles at me. He lets go of my shoulders and starts talking to Will about some other friends.

I glance at the clock behind the checkout counter. Stretching class starts in four minutes. I didn't time the trip to the store, but it had to be at least that long. I shift my weight from foot to foot, but Braedon doesn't look ready to go anytime soon.

"So, hey, I'm going to head back," I finally say as I put my Coke on the nearest shelf.

Braedon doesn't hear me. He and Will keep talking.

I look at the clock again. Eleven o'clock exactly. I can picture everyone lined up for class. And Mom wondering where in the world I am. I take a step toward the door, hoping to hint to Braedon that we have to go, *now*.

"Just a sec, Kaitlin. Gotta pay for my Coke." Braedon fishes some change from the pocket of the hoodie he's carrying and hands it to the clerk.

I push the door open, the little bell jingling through the store.

"Catch you later, B," Will says. They slap hands, and Braedon finally follows me.

I sprint down the sidewalk, hoping to make up for lost time. The late-summer breeze hits me from behind, as if it's pushing me along.

"Wait up." Braedon jogs a little to catch up, then takes a swig of his Coke. "What's the hurry?"

I slow to a fast walk. "We're going to be late."

"To stretching class?" He laughs. "Who cares? It's not actual ice time."

My mom cares, but I don't say that to Braedon. It sounds so . . . babyish. Plus, I kind of want to go to stretching class. I was hoping it would help me get a higher spiral.

As we turn to enter the parking lot of the rink, Braedon stops me.

"Look, Kaitlin, I'm sorry. It's important to you, isn't it?"

I shrug and wipe some sweat from my forehead.

"I wasn't really thinking. Next time, I promise not to get distracted. Forgive me?" He puts on a little pout.

Next time. Is he saying we'll do this again? As nervous as I am about walking into the rink and facing Mom, my insides go warm.

"Forgiven," I say. Since I can count my friends on one hand, I can't really stand to lose any of them.

I thrust open the door and take a deep breath.

Chapter Thirteen

I push the mashed potatoes across my plate and listen to Mom go on and on about how I acted irresponsibly. I didn't put my skating career first, and I take my parents for granted. Which I don't at all, but I know that Mom sees being even a little late to class differently.

I try to swallow some potatoes. They stick in the back of my throat. I actually don't even like mashed potatoes unless they have gravy, but Mom never makes gravy.

"Don't you agree?" Mom asks Dad.

Dad's busy chewing and makes some vague sound.

Mom turns back to me. "I don't understand why you didn't

simply ask. I'm not against you doing things with friends. But disappearing without saying anything is unacceptable. When you weren't there at the start of class, I was worried sick. I didn't know where you were. And you *know* better than that, Kaitlin."

Mom's words gnaw at my core. I should've told her where I was going. "I'm really sorry I made you worry."

"I can't believe I have to do this again so soon." She holds her hand out for my phone.

I slide it out of my pocket and give it to her. Big deal. I haven't heard from Ellery in days. Miyu's mom won't let her have a phone. And Braedon . . . my face flushes a little. He doesn't even have my number. I wonder if he wants it.

"Kaitlin, is everything all right?" Mom's voice is quieter than normal.

I nod and try to make my mashed potatoes disappear under the chewed cob of corn.

"You've just been acting so strangely. Not like yourself at all."

"I'm fine," I say. She makes it sound like I have a disease or something.

Mom sighs. "No computer except for schoolwork, no TV, and bed at nine o'clock. Got it?"

"Yes," I mumble.

"You need to straighten up. Fallton is your last chance. Don't throw it away. Your focus should be on this new program and what you need to do at Regionals. Nothing else. We're paying too much money for you not to take this seriously."

I sneak a glance sideways at Dad. He winks at me. If he was the one at the rink with me every day, I doubt he'd get so worked up about a quick trip to the store and being a few minutes late to class.

"How was the dance class?" Miyu asks on Monday morning as we lace up our skates.

"The class was okay. I tried to work it into my program, but Greg kept going on about using the 'feel' of the tango but not the actual tango. I wish I knew what he meant." I double-knot my right skate and do a quick glance around the lobby. "Oh, and Addison showed up."

"Seriously? I bet it was her mom's idea. She probably couldn't stand the thought of another skater having an advantage over her baby."

I giggle as I think of Mrs. Thomas snapping photos with her phone. But then I kind of feel a little bad for Addison too, even though it's clear she hates me.

"Anyway, I was going to tell you all about that on Saturday.

Were you sick?" I ask. Miyu didn't show up for the Saturday morning practice sessions.

She shakes her head as she pulls guards onto her blades. "No, I had academic team tryouts. And I got in!"

Oh, right. School starts this week for all the normal kids whose moms aren't afraid that going to real classes will destroy their skating careers. "Congratulations," I tell her. "I wish I could do something like that."

"Like what? Academic team?"

"That. Or just going to school." I tug the ankles of my tight skating pants down over the tops of my boots.

"Have you told your parents you want to go to school?" Miyu asks.

Clearly Miyu has not spent much time with my mother. I sneak a look to make sure she's far enough away not to overhear. "No way. Mom would flip out. First, she'd say no. Then she'd launch into a lecture about how homeschooling is so much better for me and my skating. Then, somehow, that would lead to a talk about how she gave up her career for me. And about how Dad works so hard to pay for my skating. And—"

Miyu holds up a hand. "Okay, okay! Your mom is crazy."

"So, now you see why I can't talk to her about school. I just have to suck it up and deal with it." I stand up, pull my favorite pair of black-and-purple-striped gloves from my bag, and sniff them. They smell like feet. I throw them back into the bag and shuffle through everything until I find a pair of pink ones I hardly ever wear.

"But she'll never know you want to go to school unless you say something." Miyu pushes through the doors, and we join a few other skaters waiting for the Zamboni to finish the ice. "I think it's better to mention it than to never say anything."

"Maybe." Miyu doesn't get it. Most things I think in my head, I can't say to Mom.

"What a waste of time," a voice says from behind us. Addison, of course. "No serious skater goes to school full-time."

"What are you talking about? I'll see you every day in English, science, and PE," Miyu says.

"Just till the end of the year. Then I'm homeschooling."

"Jessa went to school. She graduated this year," I say, remembering a random fact I read in a skating magazine.

"And Jessa completely lost it at Worlds, remember? Too much stress." Addison looks as if she's ready to go to Worlds herself in her brilliant black-and-white dress covered in crystals and her hair freshly dyed and pulled into a bun. "It's my dress for Regionals," she says when she catches me staring.

"Oh. It's pretty." The Zamboni chugs toward the garage door. I wish it could do more than two miles an hour, just so I could get away from Addison.

"What's your dress look like? Oh, wait, you just got a new program. Guess you don't even have a dress yet," Addison says. "You better hurry, because you won't get one custom-made in time."

"I'm sure Greg's thought of that," Miyu says.

I realize Addison's right. There's no way my soft-pink *Swan Lake* dress will work for this crazy tango program. There are less than six weeks until Regionals. I know because I'm marking the days off on a calendar at home. Every big black *X* gets me one day closer to the competition that will decide the rest of my season. I'd be lucky to order a dress and even have it show up on time, never mind get it fitted and test it out on the ice. What am I going to wear?

The dress is the first thing on my mind when I find Greg for my lesson.

He waves a hand. "No problem. I'm sure we can find one for you. One of the ice dancers should have a tango dress, and we can get someone to shorten it to free skate length. Now, let's run through the program." He snaps his fingers at the ice monitor.

A used dress. Great. Another reason for Addison to laugh at me.

I stop in the middle of the ice and wait for the music to start. Braedon glides by and waves. I grin at him and wonder if he got grounded too. Somehow I doubt it.

The tango music begins, and I go through the motions of the program. When it stops, I'm completely out of breath, but I did everything right.

"That's a start," Greg says. "Now we have to make it a tango."

By the end of the lesson, my whole program is full of arm movements and facial expressions and even more little things to do between the jumps and spins. I run through it over and over again until I have everything committed to memory.

Remembering it all isn't too bad. But actually doing every little wrist flick and head tilt while still landing the jumps . . . that's the part I'm not completely sure I can do.

When I reach the lobby after the session, Mom's staring at something intently on her phone.

"Look at this." She holds out the phone. "I recorded your new program so you can watch it at home."

I glance at the screen. There I am, stumbling after Greg as he twists and turns and calls out, "Double flip here" and "Then stop and flirty pose." Except for the jumps and the spins, I look like a total beginner. How in the world am I ever going to get this program down before October? Maybe it's good Mom taped it. I can study it over and over. There's no way I'm going to Regionals with a messy program, even if it is to music that's so not me.

"Thanks, Mom! That'll really help."

She beams at me. She and Greg think I can do it. I wish I felt the same way.

Chapter Fourteen

Ever since Miyu and I talked about going to school earlier in the week, it's been weighing on me like a pair of skates around my neck. Obviously, there's no way I can ask Mom about it.

But I can always talk to Dad.

I make it through my tango class. At least this time I got to partner with the bored-looking guy instead of Addison. We worked on these little twisty steps called *ochos*, which were actually a lot of fun, and I think I can work them into my program. Although working dance moves into my program didn't go so well last time. But what's the point of me taking this class if at least *some* of it doesn't get into my skating?

After dinner, Mom heads upstairs to lie down. I follow Dad into the family room. He sits on the couch, picks up the remote, and turns on a sports channel where some big, thick-necked guys are discussing Michigan football's upcoming season.

I sit on the couch, cross-legged, so I'm facing him. I swallow and make myself say it. "I . . . want to talk to you about something."

Dad gets that look on his face like I'm about to ask him about my period. He turns down the TV volume. "What is it, Pumpkin?"

What if he says no? Or worse, what if he thinks I need to bring it up with Mom? I try to remember what Miyu said. If I don't tell them, they'll never know. I fix my eyes on Dad's shiny bald spot. Why doesn't he just shave the ring of brown hair around it? It's like he can't bear to let that last little bit of hair go.

"Kaitlin?"

Still looking at the bald spot, I let out my breath and just let it spill. None of my words sound very persuasive, and I'm sure he's going to say no. I finish and force my eyes to meet his soft brown ones. One of my hands is stuffed behind the couch cushion. I find a penny and rub it between my fingers for good luck. Then I drop it and cross my fingers instead.

"This is something you really want, isn't it?" he says. "To go back to school?"

I look him right in the eyes and nod. "More than anything. Sometimes . . . never mind."

"Sometimes what?"

"It sounds silly, because I go to the rink every day, and I have you and Mom. But I guess I get a little lonely sometimes." I sound really pathetic, but it feels kind of good to finally let the truth out.

Dad tilts his head. "I thought you might be." He pauses. "I doubt your mother will go for it."

"I know. She'll think I won't have enough time to practice." My fingers uncross. I should've known this wouldn't help. I stand up and move toward the hall.

"I'll talk to her," he says just as I'm about to leave the room. "I can't promise it'll work, but I'll say something."

I race back to the couch and throw myself at him in a hug. He makes a noise like a balloon that's been pricked, and I laugh.

I run up the stairs two at a time. I can't wait to tell Miyu.

———·····———

"I knew it would work!" Miyu says at the rink on Saturday morning.

"It probably won't. But at least I said something, and now Dad knows how I feel." I sip some water and keep an eye out for Greg.

"But if he's all for it, you have a chance. Be optimistic, Kaitlin." Miyu bumps me with her elbow, and water dribbles down my chin.

I wipe it off with my pink-gloved hand and see Greg motioning at me for my lesson. "Gotta go," I say.

"Wait! A bunch of us are going out tonight. Food, maybe a movie. Want to come?"

Yes! I want to shout. I picture Ellery and all her friends from school, laughing and having a good time at the pizza place. Only with me instead of Ellery. "Sure," I say like it's no big deal. "I'm ungrounded as of yesterday. Let me ask my mom."

Greg's full-force into tangoing this morning. I show him the *ochos*, which he actually likes and works into the very beginning of the program. I run through the whole thing—with *ochos*, which are maybe even more fun to do on ice. Braedon winks at me as I finish the footwork at the far end of the rink, and I almost trip over my toe picks. I barely squeak out the double axel at the end, but at least I land it. I stop and pose as the last note echoes through the rink.

"You've got the elements down," Greg says as I gulp water. He has his gloves off and is slapping them against his hand. "Good work on the double axel at the end. I know that's not easy. And those new steps at the beginning look great."

I eye him over the top of my water bottle. There's something he's not saying. Some "but."

"But . . . ," I provide for him.

"There's still no spark. No connection to the music. Not yet."

I groan inside my head. How am I supposed to connect with music that's so . . . flirty?

"And that's what we're going to work on today. Because you're competing at the Chicago Invitational over Labor Day weekend."

My water bottle slips from my grasp. I grab it from the ice and set it on the boards. "I'm competing . . . what?"

"Everyone here goes. You'll have company," Greg says, as if this is what I'm worried about. "I already talked to your mom about it. She thinks it's a good idea."

"But that's next weekend!"

"Then we'd better get this program polished to star quality before then."

Chapter Fifteen

After my lesson, I work extra, super hard. There's no way I'm going to Chicago and looking like I just got my program. Which I did, of course, but I don't want to look like it.

I finish the gazillionth run-through of my footwork sequence and analyze the tracing of the bracket turn I just did.

"Kaitlin?"

I run my blade over the line I made on the ice. It's flat and straight, instead of curved like it should be. I'll have to work on that.

"Hello? You've been doing that footwork over and over. What's going on?" Miyu holds out my water bottle.

"Thanks." I grab the water and drink like I've never had water before. It's funny how water can taste like the best thing ever when you're really thirsty. "I'm competing in Chicago."

"Me too! I'm glad you're going."

I shrug and squint at the lines on the ice again, trying to figure out how to fix my brackets.

"You don't want to go," she says.

"I'm not ready. Like, I know it's important to compete the new program before Regionals, but what if I can't *do* it?" Saying those words out loud is beyond scary.

"Kaitlin, you work harder than anyone else here. If you want it, you can do it," Miyu says.

I smile. "Thanks. Greg keeps asking me things like, 'Where's the emotion? Where's the heart?' and telling me I have to feel the music, whatever that means. Sometimes I think the entire thing is just going to be this huge disaster, and maybe I just should've stuck to *Swan Lake*."

"I know what you need," Miyu says. "Time on the ice that's not practice. Just fun. Let's stay and do the public skate."

I bite my lip to keep from smiling too much. I never knew what I was missing when I thought Ellery was my friend. Miyu always seems to know exactly the right thing to do. I check with Mom, even though I know she'd never say no to more skating time.

I haven't been to a public session in years. I forgot how crowded it is. People cling to the boards to stay upright, and kids chase one another and crash everywhere on the ice.

Music blares from the speakers—music people actually listen to, not the classical pieces we use for our programs. And it's loud. Really loud. People shout across the ice at one another, scream when they fall, and sing along to the music. One girl is doing some kind of dance on her brown rental skates to the song playing, her friends watching and laughing.

"This is insane," I say to Miyu as we quickly maneuver around a guy who's just fallen in front of us.

"I know. Isn't it great?"

"Yeah." And I mean it. "No one here cares about landing jumps or qualifying for Nationals or whether their mom thinks they're wasting their time."

"I wish someone would tell Addison that." Miyu nods toward the middle of the ice.

Addison's plugging away at her own footwork, a determined look on her face. I glance toward the bleachers, knowing what I'll see there. Sure enough, Mrs. Thomas is camped out, watching her daughter's every move. I half expect her to leap onto the ice with a camera, the way she did at the dance class.

"I know Addison hates me, but I kind of feel bad for her. Like her mom is making her practice," I say.

Miyu watches Addison for a moment. "I know. Let's go make her loosen up."

"How?" I ask, but Miyu's already gliding around other skaters to get to the middle.

"Hey, Addison," she says.

Addison stops mid-turn. "What do you want?"

"To challenge you to a friendly competition." Miyu smiles.

"How is that going to loosen her up?" I whisper in her ear.

Addison's eyes bore into me. "Are you talking about me?"

I shift in my skates and pull on my new club jacket. "Um . . . no . . ."

"I can beat both of you at any competition." Addison's talking to Miyu, but she's only glaring at me.

Miyu taps a finger on her chin like she's thinking really hard about the perfect challenge. "How about a spin-off?"

"What's that?" I ask.

"You don't know anything, do you? You start with a basic spin. The next person adds a different position, the next person adds something else, and on and on until someone falls over or messes up the order." Addison explains this to me like I'm some little kid who asked her how to skate backward.

"So, are you in?" Miyu asks her.

Addison glances up at her mom in the stands. "Of course I'm in. I'm a better spinner than either one of you. But only if Miss Klutz doesn't punch me in the nose while she tries to keep up."

"That was an accident," I say, but Addison's already doing tiny back scratch spins, rotating on the ice with her left foot crossed in front of her right. I flash back to my first week at Fallton, when Addison copied what I was doing, and I completely crashed on that sit spin combo. At least now I know what to expect from her.

Addison stops spinning long enough for a round of Rock, Paper, Scissors to see who starts. Miyu's paper smothers our rocks. Addison and I stand on either side to keep anyone from running into her while she spins. Miyu does a perfect camel, her arms outstretched and her right leg lifted high behind her as she spins around and around.

She finishes with a flourish. "Next!"

I take her place and do the camel, then crouch down into a sit spin.

"Easy," Addison says as I exit the spin.

"Do I see a spin-off?" Braedon skids to a stop, spraying ice all over Miyu's tights.

She swats the ice off her legs. "You're not invited."

"Miyu . . . ," I start to say. She's the last person I'd expect to be so mean.

"It's okay. She doesn't like me. Though I don't know why." Braedon sticks out his bottom lip in a mock pout. "I know Kaitlin's glad to see me." He punches me lightly on the arm, and it feels like molten lava is spreading through my body.

Addison's eyes flick from me to Braedon. "Why can't he join? It'll be fun. Who put you in charge anyway, Miyu?"

"We've already started, and he's a level ahead of all of us," Miyu replies.

"But I'm awful at spinning," Braedon says.

If he doesn't like to spin, then there has to be some other reason he wants to join us. I can't help but hope it's because he wants to hang out with me.

"Fine." Miyu sighs. "You go after Addison."

Addison shoots a smile at Braedon and starts spinning. She adds a layback after the sit spin, arching her back until she can almost see behind herself as she spins. Her arms form a perfect circle and her right leg is extended back and just slightly bent. "Good luck with that," she says to Braedon after she finishes.

I wonder how in the world Braedon's going to pull off a layback. Guys hardly ever do them.

"Just watch." And he does it—sort of. He sticks his leg out at an awkward angle behind him and tilts his head back.

Addison dissolves into giggles. "That's the worst layback I've ever seen!"

"Not cool!" he shouts as he does some weird thing with his leg out to the side and his body leaning the opposite direction.

"What kind of spin is that?" Miyu asks.

"I call it the Braedon," he says.

"That's a perfect name." Addison's smiling more than I thought was possible for her.

Then I realize she's been smiling almost nonstop since Braedon showed up. It's like the pieces of a puzzle have just fit together in my head. Addison likes Braedon. And I really hope he doesn't feel the same way about her.

We go around and around, adding to the spin and getting dizzier with each turn.

"We have an audience," Braedon says as Addison goes through the motions of our crazy spin.

Sure enough, there's a circle of kids standing around us, watching Addison twirl away. She ends with an I-spin, her left leg practically touching her cheek in perfect splits. The kids around us clap. Addison ends with her arms gracefully outstretched and flashes a smile to everyone.

"Always performing," Miyu whispers in my ear.

"Okay, *that's* not fair," Braedon says to Addison. "You know I can't do that."

"Then I win!" Addison jumps up and down on her toe picks.

"And I challenge all of you to a jump-off," Braedon says.

"I don't know. . . ." Miyu glances around the rink. "It's really crowded. There's not enough room."

"Are you afraid I'll win?" he asks.

"Of course not," Miyu says.

"I'm in," Addison says.

"Me too." I look at Braedon. "You know I'm a jumping machine, right? There's no way you'll beat me." If I'm confident about anything, it's jumps.

"You're on, Double Axel."

I turn to Miyu. "C'mon, please? We'll be careful about where we jump. It won't be as good without you."

"It does sound fun. . . ." Miyu surveys the crowd again.

I put my hands together like I'm praying.

Miyu rolls her eyes at me, but she's smiling. "Okay, fine. But only jumps that all of us can do are allowed. Meaning no double axels or triple sals, Braedon. And it doesn't count if one of us has to stop jumping to avoid hitting someone."

"Sounds good," Braedon says. "I'll start."

"Wait . . . ," Miyu says, but Braedon's already flying down the ice, weaving around little kids and their parents.

"Watch this!" he shouts.

"That's too fast. He's going to run someone over." Miyu stands on her toe picks to try and see him.

I clench my hands as Braedon does a perfect double flip at the end of the rink.

The kids standing around us ooh and aah.

"That's nothing." Addison flips her ponytail over her shoulder and pushes off. She circles the rink a couple of times, spots an empty corner, and does a double flip and then a single loop with her arms over her head, jumping up and landing on the same foot.

"Awesome!" a kid next to me says.

"Show us what you've got, Double Axel," Braedon yells across the ice.

I smile at him and take off. I pass a big group of ten-year-old girls with HAPPY BIRTHDAY ASHLEY T-shirts, doing their best to stay upright. I dart to the left to miss hitting a teenager in hockey skates, and then to the right to get around a mom and dad holding their little daughter up between them.

"Kaitlin, here!" Miyu shouts from behind me.

I do a quick glance and see the area where she's pointing, just past the middle of the rink. I gather speed, turn backward, and pick in for the double flip just after I pass my friends. I land it easily, add the single loop with my arms over my head—which isn't so easy—then step forward and leap up into a single axel. As I turn one and a half times in the air, Miyu shouts something. The jump moves so fast, I don't have time to see what she's yelling about.

But I find out when I land on top of one of the Happy Birthday Ashley girls.

Chapter Sixteen

"Oomph!" My breath rushes out as I crash into her. We both fall in a tangled mess of limbs and skates. I roll off her and sit up as fast as I can. My right elbow is throbbing where it made contact with the ice. I bend it. At least nothing's broken.

"Are you okay?" I ask the girl with blond hair and braces lying next to me on the ice.

"Uh . . ." is all she says as one of her friends helps her sit up.

"Kaitlin!" Miyu scrapes to a stop beside me, Braedon and Addison right behind her.

"I'm fine," I say. "Just bruised."

Braedon reaches out a hand to help me up.

"I saw her at the last minute and tried to warn you, but it was too late." Miyu peers around me. "She's bleeding."

I spin around to see the girl still sitting on the ice, her face turning white as she watches blood spread into the knee of her jeans.

"I'm so sorry," I say. "I didn't see you."

The girl gives me a half smile. Her friend glares at me. "Isn't it illegal to do crazy stuff like that when there are people who don't know how to skate?"

"I—I'm sorry."

Miyu touches my arm. "Kaitlin didn't mean to hurt anyone. It was an accident."

"We need to get you inside," Braedon says to the girl. "Can you hold on to me and stand up?"

Two men push Braedon aside. "We'll take her in," one of them says. They must be fathers of a couple of the girls in the birthday group. They aren't even wearing skates—just sneakers. They carefully pull the girl up and carry her into the lobby.

"I can't believe that happened. What if she's not okay? What if she's hurt really bad?" I pull on the fingers of my stupid pink glove. Maybe if I was wearing my good striped gloves, this wouldn't have happened.

"She'll be fine. You just nicked her shin with the back of your blade," Braedon says.

"She was bleeding!" There's an edge to Miyu's voice.

"Please. It's not like blood was gushing out all over the place." Addison twirls the end of her ponytail with her index finger as she looks up again at her mom in the stands. Mrs. Thomas is making this circular motion with one of her fingers, universal Skate Mom speak for *Stop talking and go practice.* "This is boring. I'm going back to my footwork."

"Haven't you done that to yourself before?" Braedon asks Miyu. "Like when you land a jump and you don't pull your leg around fast enough?"

"That doesn't matter. That girl wasn't a skater. She didn't come here expecting to get a blade to her leg." Miyu's hands are on her hips. She looks ready to start World War III with Braedon.

Braedon's about to say something else, but I cut him off. "Hey, let's go check on her," I say to Miyu. I give Braedon a quick smile before skating off with Miyu toward the doors. He grins at me, and I go warm all over.

"I should've known that something bad would happen

when he showed up," Miyu says as we step onto the rubber mats. "It was his stupid idea to have a jump-off. I don't know why I went along with it."

"He just likes to have fun," I say. "It's more my fault than anyone's, since I'm the one who ran into her."

But Miyu's right about one thing. Trouble seems to follow Braedon.

Mom talks nonstop about the Chicago Invitational while she drives me to Pizza Supreme to meet everyone from the rink. When we finally get there, she says, "I'll be back to pick you up after the movie. Nine thirty on the dot. No later. You need your sleep. And don't forget to have a salad with your pizza."

I give her a kiss on the cheek and jump out of the car. When I open the door to the restaurant, I spot Miyu with a bunch of other kids in a booth near the back. Across from her is a guy with brown, swishy hair. Braedon.

Miyu spots me and waves. She scoots over and I sit next to her.

"Hey, Double Axel," Braedon says in his smooth voice.

I can't help the smile that creeps across my face.

"More like Klutzy Kaitlin." Addison's sitting to Braedon's right. She giggles like she's made the best joke in the world.

"Hey, Addison, I'm glad your mom let you out on your own for the night," Miyu says with a fake smile.

"What does that mean?"

"She usually watches every move you make, doesn't she?"

Addison narrows her eyes. "At least she cares. I've never seen your mom at the rink."

"That's because she works for a living." Miyu sips her drink.

"Oh. So that's why you've worn the same dress to every competition since last year," Addison says with an innocent lift of her eyebrows.

"Quit being rude, Addison," Jessa Hernandez says from the corner of the booth. "Everyone already knows about your four hundred dresses with ten million Swarovski crystals."

"Kaitlin, did you meet this weirdo yet?" Braedon nods toward the guy sitting across from Jessa.

"Tom," the weirdo who doesn't look so weird says. Although he does look a little like a Q-tip, with his pale skin and blond buzz cut.

I recognize him as half the ice dancing team I saw doing all the crazy moves. "I've seen you at the rink."

"Samantha and I just got back from training camp at Lake Placid," Tom says.

"Really? That sounds cool."

He runs a hand through his almost nonexistent hair. "It was brutal."

"Tom and Samantha are the best dance team in the state," Addison purrs. "Not that Kaitlin would know. She's going to take beginner dance lessons with Svetlana."

I kind of wonder if Addison will show up and crash my ice dance lesson the way she did the tango class. "I've taken dance before. It's just been awhile. My old coach wanted me to focus on freestyle."

Addison puts on a super-serious face. "That makes sense. No offense, but it's obvious in tango class that you aren't a natural dancer."

Okay, I know I'm not that great, but I'm definitely not any worse than Addison. Miyu's glaring at Addison. I clench my hands together and try to think of a good comeback.

"Need a partner?" Braedon gives me a half smile. "I'm always free for tango. Especially in a parking lot."

I laugh a little too loudly and gulp ice water before Braedon can see how red my face is.

"So . . ." Addison shifts her gaze from me to Braedon. "What kind of pizza are you getting? Pepperoni? You look like a pepperoni kind of guy."

"Actually, I can't eat pizza crust," Braedon says as he studies the menu. "I'm allergic to wheat. I have to order crustless pizza."

Miyu elbows me. It looks like she's biting the inside of her cheek to keep from laughing.

"You are, really?" Addison's practically simpering. "That sounds awful."

"My pizza doesn't even look like a pizza anymore. It's just a pile of melted cheese, toppings, and some sad-looking sauce oozing out." Braedon's looking Addison right in the eye.

I shift in my seat and pull the menu up in front of my face. Hmm . . . pineapple and black olive pizza or . . .

I peek around the menu. Addison's giving him flirty eyes. The kind of eyes Greg keeps telling me I need to do in my program. Except she's really good at it. I try to memorize the look for my next lesson. Then I notice Addison's hand on Braedon's arm. Something sour rises from my stomach, and I feel the need to jump across the table and pry her hand away.

But I don't. I just peer at them from around my menu until I hear a funny noise from down the table. Jessa's hands cover her mouth, but little strangling sounds come out.

Miyu grins at me. I look around the table, and everyone—except Braedon and Addison—looks as if they're about to burst into laughter. I'm trying to figure out what's so funny when the waiter shows up.

"Hey, y'all," he says in a Southern accent. "Ready to order?"

"Split my pineapple and black olive?" Miyu asks me.

I nod. "That's my favorite." I've never met anyone else who likes pineapple and black olive pizza.

"Mine too."

"Can I have the Mega Meat pizza, with extra meat and thick crust?" Braedon hands his menu to the waiter.

I stare at Braedon. Didn't he just tell Addison he couldn't eat pizza crust?

"What's going on?" Addison asks as the whole table—except me and her—cracks up. "I don't get it."

"He's not allergic to wheat," Tom says.

"Then why did you say you were?" she asks Braedon.

"Because it was a good joke . . . and you seemed so concerned," he says through laughter.

I start to laugh too. Mainly because of the ticked-off look on Addison's face.

"It's not funny," she says. That just makes everyone laugh harder.

Braedon catches my eye and smiles. I feel kind of funny myself. Not like funny ha-ha, but tummy butterflies funny. I rearrange my silverware on the red-and-white plastic tablecloth and don't look at him again.

Miyu pokes me with her elbow again. "Hey, I have to go to the bathroom. Come with me?"

I follow her through the bright yellow door labeled LADIES and wait at the mirror, trying to push some stray hairs into place.

"So, what's going on between you and Braedon?" she asks me as she washes her hands.

"What? Nothing! He's my friend, I guess." I decide to wash my hands too. Maybe that will stop them from shaking.

"Seriously, Kaitlin. I saw the way he looked at you. And you've been spending a lot of time with him."

"Not really." I scrub at my fingernails.

"He's a fun guy, but you should know he's not serious about anything at all. Not skating, not school, not friends."

I remember what Braedon said the other day to that guy at the convenience store, about how he'd been kicked out of his school.

"That stupid jump-off thing—remember how he barely cared when that girl got hurt? You could've been really hurt too. And before that, you told me you were late to stretching class because of him. I haven't known you long, but you've never been late to anything skating-related."

"It wasn't that big of a deal," I say, although part of me is happy that Miyu cares enough to tell me what she thinks. It's nice to have a friend like that, for a change.

"Just be careful is all."

Back at the table, I sort of listen while the others talk. Addison tries to tell everyone about her new dress, but she's cut off by Tom and Braedon flicking balled-up straw wrappers at each other. Braedon aims one at Addison, and it lands in her pizza. Braedon's hair hides half his face, and I wonder if Miyu is right. Is he trouble? Does it even matter? After all, we're just friends. It's not as if he's my boyfriend or anything.

Like Mom would ever let me have a boyfriend.

". . . won't be as bad as Regionals, though." I tune in halfway through whatever it is Jessa's saying.

"What won't be as bad as Regionals?" I ask.

"The things people say at competitions," Jessa says. "You know, 'Fall Down' and stuff like that. At one of the summer competitions, someone told me to retire already." She picks at her pizza.

"Really?"

Jessa nods but doesn't look up.

"They catch us in the hallways or the locker rooms. Sometimes right by the ice as we're waiting to go on," Miyu says.

I think back to Praterville and other competitions. I've never heard anyone say something so mean to another skater. Usually we're all just too focused on ourselves to do anything except give one another nervous smiles, or maybe say, "Good job" when someone comes off the ice.

"And don't forget the stuff that randomly goes missing," Tom adds. "A couple of years ago, Samantha's skates disappeared. We found them just in time, hanging over one of the stall doors in the men's bathroom."

"Someone took my warm-up sweater at Praterville," Miyu says.

"Seriously?" I've heard stories about things going missing, but never actually had it happen to me or anyone from Ridgeline. Well, one time Ellery lost a hair ribbon and insisted someone had stolen it, but I'm sure she just dropped it in the parking lot or something. "This stuff really happens?"

Everyone stares at me like I'm crazy.

"It only happens to us," Jessa finally says. "They single us out."

"Why?" I ask.

"Do you have to ask?" Tom says. "We skate for Fall Down. Why else?"

"You guys take this all way too seriously," Braedon says through a mouthful of pizza. "Once, someone stole my skate laces. So I went through everyone's stuff in the locker room, took something from each of their bags, and lined it all up on one of the vendors' tables out in the lobby."

Addison laughs way too loudly at this. I guess she's forgiven Braedon for pretending to be allergic to wheat.

"But not everyone stole your laces. How does that make sense?" Miyu asks.

Braedon shrugs. "It doesn't. But it was really funny. And no one ever took anything from me again."

After we pay for the pizza and start toward the movie theater, Jessa walks with me. "Just make sure you lock everything away in Chicago," she says. "It probably won't be as bad as Regionals, but why take a chance? And wear earbuds while you wait to go on the ice. That way you can't hear what anyone else says."

I nod, but inside I feel a little sick. It can't be that bad. If it was, I would've heard about it, right?

Chapter Seventeen

Mom's still going on and on about Chicago while I'm lacing up my skates Monday morning.

"Of course you'll be ready," she says after I tell her I'm not sure if three weeks is long enough to have a new program down. "Greg knows what he's doing."

"But I just feel weird with the music," I say as I loop the extra lace around my boot hooks. I'm wondering if I should've chosen not to do the new program. Maybe I could've proved him wrong by skating to *Swan Lake* and winning Regionals.

"What do you mean, weird?"

I shrug. "I don't know. It just doesn't feel very 'me.'"

"That doesn't even make sense. You don't have to be you. You're performing. You can be anyone or anything."

"I guess." In a way, I know Mom is right. Even though I get to do a lot of fun things in the new program, the tango music and all the new flirty moves just make me feel . . . uncomfortable. Add that to all the stuff everyone told me about what might happen at the competition, and I can't help but feel nervous already.

But it's too late to change my mind now. I promised Greg I'd do the best I can. Plus, he is my coach. He knows what he's doing. I'll push through it and pretend I love it. I can do the big stuff in the program, after all. I just need to figure out exactly what it is Greg's looking for to make it perfect.

"I still don't have a dress." I stand and do a few knee bends to make sure my laces are tight, but not too tight.

"I talked to Greg about that. He said Samantha has one we can use." Mom thrusts my finally washed striped gloves into my hands. "It's time. Go, go, go."

I yank on the gloves, grab all my stuff, and join the ranks of yawning skaters clomping their way to the ice.

"So . . . did your dad talk to your mom about school yet? She said yes, right?" Miyu tosses her blade guards onto the boards and hops from the rubber mats to the ice. She turns around and puts her hands on her hips. "Tell me!"

"I don't think he's talked to her. He has to wait for the right moment. And right now she's too caught up in the Chicago competition." I follow Miyu onto the ice to scrape down the bumps. "By the way, is all that stuff really true?"

"You mean what happens to us at competitions? You bet. I couldn't believe it either until it happened to me."

I want to ask Miyu more about it, but Greg calls me over for my lesson.

"Change of plans," he says.

I cross my gloved fingers and hope that means we're going back to my old program.

"Svetlana had a cancellation this morning, so you're going to get an ice dance lesson with her." He looks over my shoulder. "And here she comes."

I want to scream and yell and beat my fists on the ice. How does Greg expect me to think about ice dance when I have a competition with a brand-new program next weekend?

"Katya? Lesson," a Russian-accented voice calls from halfway across the rink. She's waiting near the ice entrance. And I guess I'm Katya.

"I'll leave you to it," Greg says before he skates off.

I cross the ice to where Svetlana is standing in the world's fluffiest fur coat, hands stuffed into the pockets—the same coat she wore my first day at Fallton. I stare at it. Is it real? And isn't she dying of heat? I mean, it *is* August, even if we are in an ice rink. All the skaters are wearing short-sleeved shirts, and even the coaches are just in light jackets.

But Svetlana doesn't look like she's even broken a sweat. As I come to a stop in front of her, my heart starts to pound. She looks a billion times stricter than Greg or Hildy. Her eyes are outlined in sharp black pencil, and the lines on her face look as if they've been there forever. Like she's never been young.

"First, we stroke." She makes a waving motion at me, so I take off.

I push around the rink, careful to keep my back straight and my knees bent, my arms relaxed and out to the sides, and my head up.

Svetlana follows me. "Point toes, Katya!"

I point my toes.

"Extend, extend!"

I extend.

"No, no! Must point toes while extend."

I point my toes while extending my leg.

"No extend to side in dance. Must extend back."

I extend straight backward.

"No! Stop." Svetlana pushes on my shoulders to make me bend my knees even more. Then she grabs my right leg and pulls it back so far, I can feel it in my hip. "Now point toes."

I point and feel a cramp in my calf.

"Yes. Do like this." She waves me off again.

I stroke and stroke and stroke, with Svetlana yelling critiques and stopping me and twisting my body into positions only contortionists can manage without pain.

"Hmm," she says.

That doesn't sound like a compliment.

"You have problems with tango, no?" she asks.

"Um. I guess."

"We work on . . ." She waves her hand in front of her face. "Face movement. You know, happy, sad, scared." Then she wiggles her finger. "But not tango, no? Tango is here." She points at my eyes. "You give eyes, you take back."

I have no idea what that means. All I can picture is holding out a pair of eyeballs to the audience. Which really seems kind of yucky.

"Is . . . how you say . . . flirting? With boy. Then no—no flirt. Flirt, no flirt."

I've never flirted. I don't even know how. "Okay," I say.

"Go on. Give best eyes to bleachers."

I look at the bleachers. "I—"

"No excuse. Make believe cute boy is there. You flirt."

I raise my eyebrows.

"Eyes. No eyebrows."

I widen my eyes.

"Hmm."

Now I know that's not a compliment.

"You need real boy." Svetlana looks around the rink. "Bretton!"

It takes me a moment to realize she's calling for Braedon. A squeaking noise comes out of the back of my throat. Braedon slides to a stop in front of us.

"What's up?" he asks.

"Katya must make the flirting. You stand here for her."

Braedon bites his lip. I can tell he's trying not to laugh. "Okay. Have at it, Kaitlin."

I feel so hot I could melt the ice. In fact, I wish I could melt *into* the ice.

"Make believe he is cute boy," Svetlana says.

"Hey," Braedon says, but Svetlana just bops him lightly on the back of the head.

I don't really have to make believe. I twist my hands together.

Braedon smirks.

"Now, Katya. You tell judges exactly how you think," Svetlana says. "Why you cannot do this?"

And why does everyone think I'm the person I was at Praterville? That was ten seconds of a huge mistake. "I just . . . I can't."

Svetlana narrows her eyes. "You think you are shy girl. But you are not. Make flirt eyes at Bretton. You will not die."

Actually, I might die. This is torture. Complete and total torture. I just have to get it over with. That's all. Then Braedon will go back to practice and my lesson will be normal again. I hope.

I drag my eyes up from my hands and lock them with Braedon's bright blue ones. I feel myself smile, and my whole body gets even warmer.

"Good!" Svetlana yells in my ear. "Now, Katya, turn away. Make believe you do not care."

That's much easier to do. I look down the ice, into the corner where Miyu is meticulously practicing double lutzes. The muscles in my face even out, and I lift my chin just a little.

"Is perfect! You do that in program for Gregor. You flirt, no flirt." Svetlana turns to Braedon. "You go now."

"Anytime," he says, punching me in the shoulder before he takes off.

I'm pretty sure I'm making flirt eyes at his back.

"So, I have a great idea," Miyu says after the session. "Are you guys coming back from Chicago Saturday night?"

"I think so. Why?" I'm totally out of breath from running my program for the zillionth time. I follow Miyu into the lobby as my heart rate finally starts to slow down.

"Can you come over Sunday night? It's Labor Day on Monday, so there's no school or skating. I'll invite a couple of friends from school and we can have a sleepover."

"Really?"

Miyu gives me a funny look. "Yeah. I'm sure my mom won't mind. She's used to having people over whenever. Ask your mom and let me know."

I practically skip in my skates over to Mom, where I sit down and wipe off my blades with an old towel. "So, um, Miyu asked if I could come over for a sleepover next Sunday. You know, since we'll be done with the competition. And there's no skating the next day."

"Miyu? Oh, right! The girl with the awful program music."

"Mom! Shh." My face goes warm, and I look around to see if anyone heard.

"Are you sure you won't be too tired from competing?"

"I can sleep in on Sunday morning. Please?" I cross my fingers under the towel, which is dripping with melted ice.

"Sure, that's fine. She seems nice enough. I knew you'd find new friends here in no time."

I'm smiling like a crazy person. I'd never even been to Ellery's house. This will be my first sleepover since . . . forever! Sunday is going to be the best night ever. I just have to get through the competition first.

Chapter Eighteen

The competition is in full swing at the rink in Chicago on Friday. Skaters run back and forth, some in warm-up clothes, others in full makeup and shimmering dresses. The vendors' booths fill the lobby from end to end, selling everything from boots and blades to stuffed animals. The muffled announcer's voice creeps in through the closed arena doors. Camera flashes light up the corner where the placement podium has been assembled. Right now, three tiny girls—all in pink dresses—are standing on places one, two, and three, grinning and holding up their medals to show their parents. And there's a table full of medals. I'm not going anywhere near that.

I've been to the Chicago Invitational twice before, so it's nothing new to me, but I feel different this time. I can't figure out why exactly. I'm standing in the middle of all of this, waiting for Mom and Dad to park the car. That's normal. I'm dragging my skate bag behind me as usual, and I have my competition dress draped over my shoulder in its plastic dry cleaner's bag. Totally normal.

A tall girl passes by with her shorter friend, and then I know what's different.

The shorter girl grabs her friend's arm and rolls up on her tiptoes to whisper in the other girl's ear. They both look right at me. Then they giggle and rush off.

I tug on my bright blue Fallton Club jacket. It seems to scream out its name, not at all like my old, subtle Ridgeline jacket. You can't help but notice it. And whisper about it, I guess.

But I'm just starting to wonder whether the girls were whispering about my new club or whether they recognized me from my Praterville outburst when Mom comes barreling through the mass of skaters and parents and coaches. Dad trails behind her, carrying the smaller bag that holds all my hair stuff and makeup.

"Why are you just standing here? Where's the sign-in?

Where's the locker room? How much time do we have before your practice? Are they running on time? Where's Greg?" The questions pour out of Mom's mouth, but she doesn't seem to be looking for any answers from me. She spots the sign-in table and heads that way. Dad and I take our time following her.

"How are you holding up, kiddo?" he asks.

I roll my skate bag back and forth across the rubber-matted floor. "Okay, I guess. Nervous."

"That's expected. Just remember that all you can do is the best you can do." Dad pats my shoulder.

Typical Dad. Nothing ever fazes him. He doesn't get that I have to do well in this competition or my chances at Regionals are pretty much shot. Gossip spreads like crazy in skating—every judge in the country probably knows about my meltdown by now. And I want to get to Nationals so badly. Last year—my first in the qualifying juvenile division—I was so close I could almost touch the shiny white ice and TV cameras.

Mom gets me registered and sends me off to the locker room while she tracks down Greg. Dad retreats to the concession stand for coffee. I find my assigned locker room and push the door open to the usual competition commotion. I slowly weave my way through girls in rhinestones and crystals, coaches giving last-minute instructions, and moms spritzing even more hair spray onto buns and ponytails. I duck around someone's extended spiral stretch and find a tiny empty space at the end of the room.

I've just put my skates on when I feel someone standing over me.

"I didn't think I'd see you here," Ellery says. She's wearing a blue practice dress and matching ribbon around her dark brown ponytail, and she's with Peyton.

"Really?" I say while pulling my own hair back. "Hey, Peyton."

Peyton glares at me. What did I ever do to her?

"I mean, with your new program and all," Ellery says.

"Oh. No, I'm skating." I gesture at the hand-me-down red dress hanging in the locker.

"It's really close to Regionals to get a new program," Ellery says. Peyton sniffs like she smells something really stinky.

"I know. I'm super nervous about it."

"I would be," Ellery says. She twirls her ponytail.

Something about the way she says that—and the way Peyton keeps glaring at me—makes my stomach twist even more. I stuff my skate bag into the locker and grab my water bottle. The sparkly one that matches the ones I made for Ellery and Peyton and all the other Ridgeline girls before Praterville.

"So, you're doing the triple salchow, right?" Peyton asks. "I mean in warm-up, just to show the judges you can do one."

Great. I forgot about all those lies I told Ellery at Pizza Supreme. "Um . . . not here. My coach wants me to play it safe."

Ellery smiles just a little, but her eyes are cold.

"Are you guys on this practice session?" I ask as I tug on the sleeves of my club jacket.

Ellery doesn't answer. She's looking at my jacket.

"So you really joined that club?" Peyton asks. She crosses her arms and raises her copper-colored eyebrows.

I glance down at my jacket. "Yeah. It's not so bad."

"Fall Down Club? Not so bad?" Ellery says with a laugh. "It's okay, Kaitlin, you can admit how awful it is."

"You've really tanked your chances now," Peyton says. "You yell at the judges and then you go join the worst club in the state."

I bite my lip. Part of me wants to tell Ellery and Peyton off the way I did the judges at Praterville. But another part of me wonders if maybe, just maybe, they're a little bit right.

"You know, it's kind of warm here." I pull off the jacket.

The second I stuff it into my locker, I feel a little sick, like I'm betraying Miyu and Braedon and everyone else at Fallton. But at least I'll be able to practice in peace, without people staring at me and whispering.

I flick the lock shut. Then I take a deep breath and follow Ellery and Peyton to the ice for practice.

I run my program over and over and try to do tango faces while still hitting all the jumps and spins. I fly across the ice, not paying attention to Ellery, and my jumps are so high I could probably do quads instead of doubles. By the end of the short practice session, I'm drenched in sweat.

"How'd it go? Ready for tomorrow?" Miyu asks as we step off the ice.

"Good. I nailed that double axel at the end every time. Maybe it will make up for how awful I am at tangoing."

Miyu gives me a smile. "You're not *that* bad at it!"

"I wish Greg felt that way," I say.

Mrs. Murakami hands Miyu her Fallton jacket.

"Where's your jacket?" Miyu asks.

I busy myself with wiping the ice from my blades and pulling on my sparkling pink-and-white guards. "I was hot."

"Really? I think this rink is way colder than Fallton.

Although I'm definitely not cold now." Miyu slings her jacket over her shoulder.

"How did your practice go?" I ask her, hoping to avoid any more talk about the stupid jacket.

"Okay. The ice is weird."

"Excuses, excuses." Braedon appears next to us, skates on and ready for the next practice session.

"Just wait till you get out there," Miyu tells him.

"If it wasn't the ice, it'd be your skates or the temperature or how many people are watching," Braedon says with a grin.

"Please, that sounds more like you. I don't complain that much. See you guys later. I have to go talk to Karilee."

"Hey, you doing anything later?" Braedon asks after Miyu and her mom disappear into the lobby. When the doors swing open, I spot Mom and Greg just on the other side, dissecting every move I made in the thirty-minute practice session. Dad's probably still at the concession stand, downing his sixth or seventh cup of coffee. If he was in charge of taking me to the rink for practice, he'd turn into coffee.

I look back to Braedon. "Not really. Dinner with my parents. Listening to my mom tell me everything I need to do to skate perfectly tomorrow." For some reason, my hands are all sweaty even though I'm not wearing gloves. I clasp them behind my back. Braedon's just a friend, that's all.

"Tom and Samantha are competing in an hour or so. Want to hang out and watch them?"

"Sure," I say, as calmly as I can. This isn't a date or anything. We're just going to sit in the freezing stands and watch people we skate with. Like friends. "Just let me run it by my parents."

"Here." He shoves his dirty black skate guards into my hands. "Hang on to these for me."

"Can't you just set them on the boards like everyone else?" Wait, why did I say that? Now it sounds like I don't want to help him out.

"Not here. Someone will steal them."

"That's crazy. I put mine on the boards and they're just fine."

"You were lucky," he says as he hops onto the ice. "It's only half an hour. Stay and watch my greatness." Then he takes off around the rink.

I don't know what else to do, so I grab the nearest seat in the third row of the bleachers, right behind a group of moms huddled under blankets and sipping coffee. After a few minutes, I begin to wish for blankets and coffee. Or maybe hot chocolate instead. Coffee kind of tastes like dirt.

The sweat on my dress has turned cold, and I'm starting to shiver. I put Braedon's guards on the seat next to me and rub my hands up and down my arms.

Braedon zips around the rink, warming up jumps and spins. Everything looks perfect. The ice monitor plays everyone's music, one at a time. When it's Braedon's turn, the music starts, exciting and loud. He lands his first jump, but then everything sort of crumbles apart. Everything except the jumps. He nearly falls out of a camel spin and trips on a footwork sequence. It hurts to even watch him. I hope he's getting the bad skate out of the way so he can do well in the actual competition.

"Is there anyone who can actually skate at that club?" A voice from the front row drifts up to me.

"He used to be a good skater. I don't know what happened," another one says.

I'm breathing as quietly as possible, as if they'll look up and notice me there. I'm pretty sure they're talking about Braedon and Fallton. I want to jump in and tell them that Braedon's a really good skater; it's just the soft ice and maybe the nerves of competition that are making him mess up.

"It's the coaches. They're just washed-up has-beens," a third mom says.

Greg is *not* a washed-up has-been, even if he is making me do this stupid tango program. My hands are shaking, as if they're talking about me. I sit on them, pushing my palms against the cool metal of the bleachers.

"You know that girl who was so rude to the judges at Praterville?" the first mom says. "I heard she's skating with Fallton now."

Great, now they *are* talking about me. I want to leave, but someone's already sitting between me and the end of the bleachers. I'd have to crawl over her to get out, and they'd definitely see me then. Instead I keep sitting on my hands and stay put. And pray they stop talking about me.

"They take in all the strays, don't they? Jessa Hernandez and all."

"I'd rather Hadley and Jason quit skating before they joined that club," the first mom says. "It's just a waste of time and money. They never win anything. They never even place."

You're wrong, I want to yell at them. *Just you wait and see!*

"Kaitlin!" Mom's voice sounds to my left, loud enough for the skaters on this side of the rink to look up. My face heats up as the chatty moms turn around.

"That's her," one of them whispers.

"Kaitlin, what are you doing? You need to stretch out before your muscles get cold."

I grab Braedon's guards, slink around the person next to me with a mumbled, "Sorry," and hop down from the bleachers.

"I'll stretch over there," I say to Mom, and point across the aisle to an empty area past the next set of bleachers. "I'm watching Braedon's guards for him."

"Why does Braedon need you to watch his guards?" Mom asks. A line appears across her forehead. "Besides, it's too cold in here. You have to get warm or you'll pull something."

I look at the clock. Ten more minutes left in the session. Plenty of time for me to stretch and run back before Braedon gets off the ice.

Mom and I find an empty corner in the hallway housing the locker rooms and offices. All down the corridor, skaters are stretching and walking through their programs. I pull my skates off and race through my stretching routine.

"Mom," I say as I hold my right foot over my head in a Biellmann position. "Can I stay to watch the dance competition? It should be done in plenty of time for dinner."

Mom beams. "Of course you can. Maybe I should stay too."

"Oh, no, you don't have to." I try to cross my fingers, but that's kind of hard when you're holding your foot over your head.

"Well . . ." Mom studies me for a couple of seconds. Something flickers across her face, but before I have time to figure it out, she smiles again. "That's fine. Now, be sure you study those high-level dance teams closely. You can learn a lot from their edging and how they hold themselves. Just wear some warm clothes. And take this blanket." She hands me the patchwork quilt she usually sits on to watch me skate. "Dad and I will check into the hotel and be back to get you around five thirty."

"Thanks, Mom! See you later." I do one last stretch, find my shoes in the locker room, and take off back to the ice.

Chapter Nineteen

"How did you get a whole locker room to yourself?" Miyu asks. The place is practically deserted. I spot a couple of girls off to the left, but that's it.

"I swear it wasn't like this before." I twirl the combination to my locker and pull out my jeans and sweater.

"Are you staying to watch Samantha and Tom?" Miyu leans against the wall and twists her silver necklace.

"Yeah," I say, kind of surprised. "Are you?"

"Of course," she says.

"I didn't think you liked dance." I toss my cold, damp

practice dress onto the bench in the middle of the aisle and pull on my warm clothes.

"I don't, but I like to cheer for my friends."

"That's really nice."

Miyu shrugs. "We all do it. It's a club camaraderie thing."

I think back to competitions, but I can't remember hearing loud cheers for Fallton skaters. I was probably too wrapped up in my own skating. I barely even hear my own parents rooting for me when I skate, never mind who's cheering for anyone else. "That's kind of cool."

"It is. We never did that at my old club," Miyu says.

"Mine either." I reach into my locker and pull out a plastic grocery store bag.

"What's that?" Miyu asks.

"I like to make things for people before big competitions. I used to make something for every girl at Ridgeline, but I'm not there, so . . ." My face goes warm. Am I being silly, making beaded bracelets for girls I've only known a few weeks?

Miyu peers into the bag. "You *made* those?"

"Um . . . yeah." I hand her a red-and-yellow one with a little gold *M* charm dangling from it. "You don't have to wear it if you don't like it."

"Are you kidding? This is awesome. And you made it in

my favorite colors!" Miyu slides the bracelet over her hand and holds it up in the light. "Thank you."

I grin. "I'm glad you like it."

"Knock-knock! Everyone decent?" Braedon's voice sounds through the crack in the locker room door. He doesn't really wait for an answer but shoves the door open and walks right on in.

"You can't be in here!" one of the girls across the room yells at him.

"Relax," Braedon says with a grin.

"Oh my God, he is seriously crazy," Miyu says to me. She points at the door and glares at Braedon. "Out! Now."

"Who died and made you boss of the skating rink?" he says. "Kaitlin, c'mon. Junior short dance is starting."

"Let's go. It's the only way to make him get out of here," Miyu says as she picks up the bag of bracelets for me.

I glance at the wrinkled Fallton jacket stuffed under my skate bag at the bottom of the locker. Miyu and Braedon are wearing theirs. I grab the shiny blue sleeve, stuff Mom's quilt into its place, and slam the door shut. Then I scurry after Miyu, who's grabbed Braedon's arm and is hauling him toward the door.

"Nice to meet you!" he shouts at the girls across the room. They just give him dirty looks.

"What is wrong with you?" Miyu demands as soon as we're out the door.

"What's wrong with you, Miss Uptight?" he says.

"You don't see anything wrong with barging into a girls' locker room?"

"Not really. Hey, you guys want something to drink?" Braedon detours toward the concession stand.

Miyu shakes her head. "I'm going out to the rink."

"Kaitlin?" Braedon asks.

I look back and forth between them. Miyu rolls her eyes at me. I kind of wish she'd be a tiny bit nicer to Braedon. "I'll see you out there," she says.

"What's your poison? Coke? Diet Coke? Hot chocolate?" Braedon asks when we reach the counter.

"Hot chocolate." I pull a five-dollar bill out of my jeans pocket, but Braedon's already passed money to the cashier.

"I'll pay," he says. "Since I'm so embarrassing and all, it's the least I can do."

"You're not embarrassing. Nothing happened." I'm really glad he didn't walk in five minutes before, when I was in the middle of changing, though. I seriously would've died of embarrassment.

"You're much cooler than Miyu," Braedon says as he hands me a cup.

"Thank you for the drink." I wrap my hands around the warm Styrofoam and walk with him out to the ice.

Braedon points to the top of the bleachers. "There they are," he says.

I follow his finger and do a double take at how many Fallton people are up there. It's practically everyone who isn't skating in the next hour and doesn't have practice scheduled on the other ice surface. Even Addison's sitting at the very top with her legs crossed, looking as bored as can be. I can't believe they're all here to cheer on two other skaters when they could be resting for their own performances. Miyu was right—this is really cool.

I ignore the voice in the back of my head that says I'm a little disappointed that it's not just me and Braedon. At least I get to sit next to him. Miyu's behind me, showing off her bracelet.

"Kaitlin made one for everybody." She hands me the bag as Jessa examines the little *M* on Miyu's bracelet.

"You did? That is *so* nice," Jessa says when I hand her a bracelet. "You're really good at this."

"Thanks." No one at Ridgeline ever got this excited about anything I made them. Even those personalized water bottles, which took forever to get just right. I give a bracelet to all the girls—except Samantha, who's competing.

Addison holds hers like it's a rotten egg.

"Um, I made it with black-and-white beads to match your dress," I tell her.

"Hmm." She rolls it onto her wrist, but doesn't say anything else.

"So where's mine?" Braedon asks.

"I only made them for the girls. I'm sorry."

He punches me lightly on the shoulder. "I'm just kidding."

The first group of dancers end their warm-up and the competition starts. I'm admiring the first girl's gorgeous dress when Addison leans forward from the end of the row above, the little silver *A* on her bracelet catching the light.

"Hey, pay attention, Kaitlin. They're doing a tango. A *good* tango," she says with a smirk.

I pretend I don't hear her, and watch the couple on the ice. She's right, though. These dancers could tango me into oblivion. The girl is giving her partner smoldering looks, ones that could melt the ice right beneath her feet. How does she do that? I grip my hot chocolate and study her face.

"Are you cold?" Braedon asks, looking at my hands clenched around the warm cup. "Here, take my jacket." Before I can say anything, he's draped his club jacket around my shoulders.

I'm sure I look even weirder wearing two bright blue Fallton jackets, but I don't say anything. Guys in romantic movies are always giving girls their coats. I can't believe how sweet Braedon is.

Out of the corner of my eye, I see Addison's leaned forward again and is throwing daggers at me with her eyes. I give her a little smile. It might be really mean, but I decide I like making Addison jealous.

"There they are!" Miyu points at the ice.

"Samantha Young and Tom Batinsky, representing Fallton Figure Skating Club in Fallton, Michigan!" The announcer's voice echoes through the rink, and everyone around me erupts into cheers.

Everyone from Fallton, that is.

"Skate great!" the whole group choruses before bursting out into wolf whistles and clapping. I join in, clapping my hands and yelling, "Woo!" Practically everyone in the rink turns to look at us except Samantha and Tom. They look deadly serious, completely in character before the music has even started.

"They should win," Jessa says as they do one last crazy-looking lift and strike an ending pose. "That was perfect."

I nod. I've never seen anything like it. Their skating was

beautiful, and their lifts and dance spins were so different from everyone else's.

"Did you *see* that last lift?" a girl sitting off to my left says to her friend. I glance toward them and recognize her from my practice session. "What was that?"

"A total disaster. And that spin where he was leaning backward? So weird."

I'm clenching my hands so hard that my nails are digging into my palms. Everyone else from Fallton is talking, so I don't think they even heard. But Braedon did.

"How can they be so mean? It was a great dance," I whisper to him.

"Told you. Everyone already has their minds made up about us. Doesn't matter how well we do. Tom and Samantha could've gone out there and skated like Meryl Davis and Charlie White," he says, referring to the Olympic gold medalist ice dancers. "And they'd still be saying all kinds of rude things."

"It's not fair." I'm thinking about those moms who were talking about Braedon earlier. And me. And about how I didn't say anything. It's like a fire is rising inside of me and is bursting to get out.

I want to say something now.

"Don't." Braedon grabs my arm just as I'm about to turn around. "It's not worth it, and you won't change their minds."

I let out a breath and face the ice again.

"Besides," he says, "you have bigger things to think about. Like proving yourself to the judges tomorrow."

The anger disappears. He's right. I have to stay focused. This is supposed to be my big comeback—a new program, a new style, a new Kaitlin. I *have* to do well here to cement my chances for Regionals. I can't give the judges any reason to score me the way they did at Praterville, which means I have to be perfect. And keep my mouth shut.

Chapter Twenty

"Everyone's so nice. Everyone from Fallton, I mean," I say to Miyu after the last of the junior dance teams skates. We're headed toward the locker room, while Braedon and everyone else stayed to watch a couple of the younger dancers in the intermediate division.

"I know. It's so different from other clubs." Miyu brushes her hand across a gorgeous yellow dress hanging near a vendor's table. "Hey, want to check out the dresses after tomorrow's qualifying round? It'll take our minds off the competition."

"Sure." We squeeze past girls stretching in the hallway,

and I push open the door to my locker room. "Hang on and let me get my stuff, and I'll walk with you to get yours."

Miyu follows me in, then stops short. "What is that?"

"What?"

"In front of your locker. Is that your dress?"

My eyes dart across the room to the bench in front of the locker I claimed. My black practice dress is balled up on the bench, surrounded by stray bits of glitter and discarded hangers. "Oh, yeah. I guess I left it out."

Miyu shakes her head and runs across the room. I'm wondering what the big deal is when she holds up the dress. A giant round hole is cut right out of the middle of it. Miyu's face peers through from the other side.

"How—what—who—" My hands are clammy, and blood is rushing in my ears.

"I *told* you not to leave anything out," Miyu says as she hands me the dress.

I run my fingers around the hole. The cut is jagged, like whoever it was did it in a hurry. "But why?"

"They hate us. Did you bring something else to wear to practice in the morning? If not, you can borrow my extra dress."

"Yeah, I have some pants." I wad up the dress and throw

it into the nearest trash can, on top of someone's half-eaten stinky tuna sandwich. "That's just so . . . mean."

"I know," Miyu says quietly. "Will your mom be mad?"

I shrug. No way will I tell her the truth. She'd complain to every competition official she could find. I'm glad I remembered to put her quilt in my locker. "I'll just tell her it tore or I lost it or something. At least it wasn't my competition dress. I can't believe I left it there."

"We were in such a hurry to get Braedon out of here, you probably just forgot." Miyu makes a face, like Braedon cut the hole himself.

"It's not his fault," I say as I get the rest of my stuff out of my locker.

"Sure. It's never his fault."

I don't say anything else, but I can't see how Miyu can pin this on Braedon. He was just being funny. He's not responsible for some awful girl cutting up my dress.

I have another good practice in the morning—this time wearing my black over-the-heel skating pants and a black top under my club jacket. No one says anything about the jacket, and I breathe a little easier—about that, at least. Miyu, Addison, and I all make it through the qualifying round—barely.

Miyu and I kill time by checking out the dresses for sale in the lobby, but neither one of us is as into it as we'd like to be. My stomach is a mess of nerves until it's time to get ready for the real competition—the championship round. Then I relax into the ritual of putting on my dress and letting Mom redo my hair and makeup.

"Hold still, Kaitlin, or I'll poke your eye out." Mom holds the eyeliner pencil dangerously close to my right eye.

Once I asked Mom why I have to wear so much makeup, and she said that if I didn't wear it, I'd be all pale and washed out on the ice. Then I asked her if I could buy some lip gloss for real life, and she said only if it's the clear kind. I'm sure this makes all kinds of sense to Mom.

Someone squeezes by and bumps my left side. The eyeliner pencil jerks up just a fraction. Mom purses her lips and lets out a frustrated sound. She puts the pencil down and picks up a bottle of makeup remover and a cotton ball.

"Is it almost done?" I ask as she pats my eyelid.

"Be patient. Beauty takes effort. And I'm trying something different from how you looked in qualifying."

I try to hold still as she finishes. After swiping on some mascara, Mom sends me to the mirror.

I weave through the crowd of skaters and moms to the

mirror over the sinks. I have to stand on my tiptoes to peer between the heads of two other girls. I finally catch a glimpse of myself in the mirror. Or what I think is myself. I barely look like me. My light brown hair is pulled back into a low ponytail, and I have this gorgeous red flower tucked into it. My brown eyes are ringed in black eyeliner and mascara, and my lips are bright red. I look at least five years older than I am. Which is weird and cool at the same time.

Miyu pushes past two younger girls and squeezes in beside me, wearing the pretty emerald-green dress she had on at Praterville. "I still can't get over how different that is from your *Swan Lake* costume," she says. "It's insane in here. Where were all these people yesterday?"

I tug on the skirt of the red-and-black dress Samantha gave me. It makes me feel really . . . bright. Like people will turn their heads just to see me walk down the hallway. I thought I might feel more comfortable after wearing it once today, but I don't. "At least it fits."

"It does more than fit," Miyu says as she examines her face in the mirror. "It looks really good."

For a hand-me-down dress, it really does fit okay—especially after the seamstress took the hem up. "It just isn't me," I say.

Miyu eyes me in the mirror. "Did you tell Greg that?"

"No. I promised him I'd make this program work. Besides, he'd say I have to get into character. You know, flirt with the bleachers, or *be* the tango, or something."

"Kaitlin! Your group is next for warm-up!" Mom shouts over the din of everyone else talking and laughing.

I'm sure my face matches the color of my dress now. You'd think I'd be used to Mom embarrassing me all the time.

"See you out there," I say to Miyu. I rush back to Mom as best I can without tripping over anyone's outstretched legs. I clear a spot to sit down and put my skates on. Mom grabs my emergency bag in case something awful happens—like a broken lace during warm-up or a last-minute music malfunction. Then I make sure that everything is in my locker this time and follow Mom toward the ice.

As we thread our way through the vendors and skaters, my heart creeps up into my throat. How will the judges react to my new program when it's up against the best skaters in my division? What if my flirty tango faces just make everyone laugh?

"There you are," Greg says as we reach the doors to the ice. "They're about to call your warm-up." We push through the doors. A cool blast from the ice mixed with Zamboni fumes hits my face. My eyes water a bit from the cold. Mom holds out my jacket, and I stuff my arms into it, thankful for the warmth. Skating dresses are designed to look good, not to keep the skater from freezing. I shove my black-and-purple-striped gloves onto my hands.

Mom leaves to join the other parents in the bleachers, and it's just me and Greg, surrounded by everyone else in my group. I wave at Miyu, who's standing with Karilee closer to the ice.

"Remember your warm-up?" Greg asks me.

"Two laps of Russian stroking, footwork, jumps easiest to hardest, and then spins," I recite.

"Will the following skaters please take the ice for their warm-up," the announcer's voice crackles over the PA system. "Ellery Goodwin, Yasmine Patel, Gemma Abbott . . ."

I don't hear the rest of the names, not even my own. I'm already on the ice, moving as fast as I can with the other girls in my group. Hildy always said that the judges start marking you unofficially in the warm-up. So you can't slack off. I hold my head up and my back straight as I pass the judges' table. My fingers tingle with nerves and excitement, and I'm already a little out of breath. I have to calm down or I'll end up passing out in the middle of the ice.

I finish the second lap, run through my footwork, and scout out a free spot to jump. I make it through all my jumps and spins, and Greg gives me a thumbs-up. The warm-up feels like it's over before it even began.

"How'd it go?" I ask Miyu as we glide toward the entrance to the ice.

She's flushed and out of breath. "Not good. Everything was messy."

I squeeze her arm. "My old coach always said that a bad warm-up meant a really good competition skate."

"I hope," Miyu says.

Just as we reach the rubber mats, Ellery swoops in front of us.

"Nice dress, Kaitlin," she says. Then she raises her eyebrows at me.

I can't figure out if that's a compliment or not. "Thanks?"

Greg and Karilee herd us into the lobby behind almost everyone else in our group. Karilee gives Miyu some last-minute instructions—something about becoming one with the ice. Miyu nods intently, like she totally gets what Karilee is saying.

"Kaitlin, focus on the music, on the emotion, just like we practiced. Don't worry about the jumps. You've got better elements than all the other girls out there. You just need to let the audience in," Greg says.

I nod and say, "Okay," but I can't seem to keep my attention on Greg. Not when Ellery and Peyton are standing right behind him, pointing to his Skating Sensation jacket and giggling. I know the show hasn't been around for years and it had things like skaters dressed as elephants, but I don't get what's so funny.

"Greg! I need to talk to you." Addison appears from the crowd, dress and makeup on, but still wearing her sneakers. Her mom trails behind her. "I can't do the combo jump at the beginning of my program. I need to—"

"Not now. We'll talk after Kaitlin's skate." Greg turns back to me.

Addison glares at me. "But I have to figure this out *now*. It can't wait."

"Yes, it can. There's another group between Kaitlin's and yours. That's plenty of time." Greg gives her a stern look, and then starts in again on how I need to listen to the music.

Addison turns in a huff and stomps back toward the locker rooms.

"Just wait until you win . . . ," her mom says, her voice trailing off as they're swallowed by the crowd.

I'm trying to pay attention to Greg's pep talk, but Ellery and Peyton are re-enacting the showdown with Addison. If I didn't know they were really making fun of Fallton, it would've been funny watching Ellery huff and puff as an exaggerated Addison. Hildy's standing off to the side, talking to Ellery's mom. I wonder if Hildy will watch me skate.

"Let's go, you're up next," Greg says.

I snap my attention back to him.

"Good luck," Miyu says as Greg and I walk toward the ice.

The skater before me finishes her program with a flourish and takes her bows. I step onto the ice while I wait for my name to be called.

My stomach feels funny, almost like I could throw up. I do a little backspin near the boards while Greg gives me last-minute instructions.

"Be strong and confident. Feel the tango. Really feel it, like we practiced," he says.

I still have no idea what he means by that, but I nod and take a sip of water. The other girl has finished her bows and glides by me on her way off the ice.

"Don't fall down," she whispers.

Greg glares at her.

My heart beats even faster. Is it possible for a twelve-year-old to have a heart attack? Miyu and the others were right. Everyone seems to hate us, and for no reason at all.

"Use that anger," Greg says. "Put it into your tango."

Easy for him to say.

"Please welcome Kaitlin Azarian-Carter," the announcer says in a booming voice. "Representing Fallton Figure Skating Club."

Chapter Twenty-One

I stroke onto the ice, holding my arms one in front and one in back as I turn to acknowledge the judges and the audience. Cheers erupt from the top of the stands. I smile as I spot Braedon, Jessa, and a bunch of other skaters from the club.

I skate to the middle and tug on my skirt. I'm sure I stand out against the ice like a rose against snow. If only I could've worn my light pink *Swan Lake* dress, even though it totally doesn't go with this program.

Actually, I wish I could just skate my old program.

But I can't do anything about that now. If I did it once today, I can do it again. I take my starting position, arms stretched out in front of me. My fingers are shaking just a little. I glance up and see people in the front row of the bleachers whispering to one another.

Probably about me.

I tilt my head down toward the ice. Then the first notes of my music start and I can't think about anything but all the little pieces that make up my program.

Arms down, flirty face, turn, stroke stroke stroke.

Footwork with the *ochos.*

Push, turn, push, act like I don't want anything to do with the imaginary guy I'm supposed to be skating with.

Layback spin. I extend my right leg behind me and arch backward until I can see the world spinning upside down.

Hop, step, turn, step, hop, hop.

Spread eagle. I open my arms as shouts and cheers from Braedon and the others rain down from the bleachers.

I land all my jumps and do all the right number of rotations on my spins. The rest of the program goes by in a blur until the double axel. I land it perfectly, and I can't help the big, not-so-tango-y grin that flits across my face.

I glide to a stop as the music finishes. Braedon's cheering louder than anyone else. I smile and curtsy to the judges and the audience, and then join Greg on the mats.

“Technically very good,” Greg says as he hands me my jacket, “but where was the feeling?”

“I tried.” I made the right faces. I don’t know what more he wants from me. A bead of sweat drips into my eye, and I swipe my forehead with my jacket.

“We’ll keep working on it for Regionals,” Greg says. “But great job on the jumps. That double axel should give you a bump up with the judges. I have to go check on Addison now.”

I smile as I picture myself with a medal around my neck, standing on the top of the podium set up in the lobby as Dad takes my picture.

Miyu and Karilee push through the lobby doors. Miyu’s face is super serious, and she keeps rubbing her hands up and down her arms.

“Hey, good luck!” I say.

“Thanks,” Miyu replies. She rubs her arms even faster. “How was your skate? I didn’t get to see it.”

“Really good, I think.”

Miyu rocks back and forth on her blade guards. “I knew you’d do fine. I couldn’t land my double lutz at all in warm-up.”

“You can do it. You just have to forget about that.”

“That’s easy for you,” Miyu says with a half smile. “Your jumps are always good.”

That's when I notice Peyton and Ellery standing back near the doors. They're pointing at Miyu and whispering something to each other. They're behind Miyu's back, and I'm glad she can't see them. I want to throw myself across the mats and shove them both to the ground. They don't know how hard Miyu practices or how much she loves to skate.

Hildy finally arrives from the lobby and shoos Peyton away. I feel a twinge of disappointment that Hildy didn't see my skate. I shove it down and turn to Miyu.

"But my spins aren't half as good as yours," I tell Miyu. "You go out there and show those judges how great you are."

"Thanks, Kaitlin," she says as she keeps rubbing her hands on her arms.

I grab her hands and squeeze them. "Breathe, and calm down."

She closes her eyes for a second and nods.

"Just skate great," I say. "We're all cheering you on." I let go of her hands and head to the stands to find Mom and Dad. I spot them sitting with a large group of Fallton skaters and parents, and I clamber up the bleachers to find a spot just below Braedon.

"Perfect!" Mom says. Dad just pats my knee and grins.

"You were awesome, Kaitlin," Jessa says from the top row. "No one else has even tried a double axel yet."

"You sure can jump under pressure," Braedon adds as he squeezes my shoulders.

"Thanks." My insides feel all warm and happy.

The announcer calls Miyu's name, and she glides out to start her program. Her music—the screechy violin piece—starts.

"She looks really nervous," Jessa says.

I cross my fingers and sit on them, pressing them into the hard metal of the bleachers.

"Relax," Braedon whispers. "You've already skated."

But I can't help it. I hope Miyu's program goes better than her warm-up.

She stumbles a little on some footwork, which makes her stiffen up. *Relax,* I think, repeating Braedon's advice to me for Miyu. If she'd relax, she'd get more knee bend, and everything would be so much easier.

But she doesn't take my silent advice. Instead she barely lands her single axel and starts traveling across the ice on her sit spin combination. I can almost see the fear on her face as she preps for her double lutz. I want to close my eyes, but I don't. Instead of going for it and falling, Miyu doesn't even try. She pops the jump to a single. At least Addison isn't here. I can't imagine what Ellery and Peyton are saying right now.

As Miyu falls on an easy double loop, I hear giggles from down below. A group of girls from another club are watching her. My hands clench into fists. How had I never noticed how rude everyone was to skaters from Fallton?

It's like I barely even knew they existed, before I became one of them.

Chapter Twenty-Two

Mom clutches her coffee and chatters away to Dad and Mrs. Murakami while we hang out in the lobby near the results wall. Almost everyone else from the juvenile division is here too. Miyu and I lean against the chilly concrete wall.

"I was awful," Miyu says. "I don't know what happened."

"Who cares about this competition? There's always Regionals," I say. It's a lie, and she knows it, but it makes her smile.

"Why is it taking so long?" Mom asks. "I thought the results were pretty clear."

Mrs. Murakami nods. "I'm sure Kaitlin placed."

Mom beams.

"You were perfect, no matter what the judges think," Dad says to me.

I smile at him. "You're supposed to say that. You're my dad."

Mom gives me a sharp look. "Now *don't* say anything to the judges if you don't place. Although I'm sure you did."

I don't want to remind Mom how wrong she was about that the last time. "I won't say a word, I promise." I've had enough of the fallout from that.

I hope I place. I don't just hope, I really, really, *really* need to get at least third place. If I do, it'll set me up for a good showing at Regionals, so long as I skate as well as I did today. The judges aren't supposed to consider previous scores, but it's hard to ignore the girls who win the big summer competitions.

"The results are coming," Greg announces as he joins us. "Have you seen Addison?"

I point across the crowd, just as the volunteer squeezes through to tape the results to the wall.

"Ready for this?" I ask Miyu.

"I guess. At least we'll know once we look, and we won't have to worry about it anymore."

"Right. Then we only have to worry about Regionals," I say.

Mom puts her hands on my shoulders. "I'm proud of you no matter what the results are. You've worked so hard with this new program."

I blink so I don't cry. Sometimes Mom says exactly what I need to hear. "Thanks," I whisper.

Addison and her mom are in front of us. Once they reach the wall, Addison does this totally dramatic turnaround.

She faces us, closes her eyes, and says, "You look, Mom. I just can't."

Addison's mom runs her finger down the list. "Ninth!" She huffs. "I knew your jumps weren't high enough. Well, you'll just have to work harder."

Addison's face crumbles.

I just stare at Mrs. Thomas. Her jaw is set, like she's never been madder in her life. I can't imagine my mom saying something that mean after a competition.

"I thought your jumps looked really good," Miyu says to Addison.

Addison swipes her face with the back of her hand. "Mind your own business," she practically hisses as Mrs. Thomas grabs her arm and pulls her out of the crowd.

Even though she's been nothing but mean to me, I can feel for her placing that low after skating a decent program. After all, I've been there before. Not to mention how awful her mom is about the whole thing.

"Dead last," Miyu says as she looks at the list. "Well, I guess I deserve it."

"You were brave to keep skating," Mrs. Murakami says. "And you'll do better next time. What do you say to some ice cream?"

I don't hear Miyu's answer. I'm too busy searching for my own name.

Which appears next to the number fourteen.

Fourteen out of eighteen girls. Five spots behind Addison.

Mom's practically sputtering. "What? Why? I never! You deserve so much better. Greg!"

Dad tries to calm her down while Greg says something to Mom about expression and feeling the music.

I just stare at the number, watching it blur as my eyes tear up. I was *good*. If this is where I place when I'm good, I don't want to know where I'd be if I was awful.

I rub my eyes with the back of my hand and squint at the scores. They gave me 23.05 for technical elements. That's better than Praterville. But the program components . . . 8.75. Worse. Much worse.

Someone pushes past me and I stand there, wondering how in the world I'm going to do better at Regionals.

Miyu puts a hand on my shoulder. "I thought you were perfect." Then she's gone, off to get ice cream, I guess. She placed worse than me, and she's trying to make me feel better. I almost want to laugh.

"Great scores, Kaitlin," Peyton says as she turns away from the list. "I guess jumps aren't everything."

"You must feel awful," Ellery adds. "Of course, I wouldn't know. I've never placed that low." She shakes her head in mock sympathy.

"Did you see that Ellery got third?" Peyton asks.

I just stare at them.

"Oh! I better get to the podium. My mom's going to want to take my picture," Ellery says.

And off they go.

"Kaitlin?" Greg says. "I'll get the protocols and see exactly where you lost points. But I'm sure it's the same as Praterville."

I kind of nod. I want to ask why. Why did I get such low marks when I've been trying so hard to make that components score so much better? But my throat is all tight, and if I say a word, I'll probably start to cry.

"I know you're disappointed," Greg says. "There's still

time before Regionals, and we'll keep working. One way or another, we'll make you a more well-rounded skater. Enjoy the rest of your weekend. I'll see you on Tuesday."

Enjoy my weekend? This is the worst weekend ever. No, maybe the second-worst. The Praterville competition has that top spot in the Horrible Weekends Competition locked.

"Come on. Our flight leaves at seven." Dad takes my arm and guides me away from the group.

"I don't understand," I whisper.

"You're always number one in my book." Dad wraps an arm around me.

Too bad dads can't determine figure-skating scores.

Chapter Twenty-Three

The reality of fourteenth place hits me, and I feel like I've been run over by a Zamboni when I let it sink in, which is the next morning.

Sunday. At least I don't have to go to the rink today.

I'm still thinking about it that evening as I get ready to go to Miyu's for the sleepover. I yank on a pair of jeans and try to figure out—for the millionth time—where I went wrong.

It feels like my skating dreams are over. That's two competitions in a row where I've scored horribly. It'll probably be the same at Regionals. And if that happens, I won't qualify for Nationals, and then my season's over. I'll do it all again next year, and for what? To get the same stupid low score? No Nationals. No Olympics.

But why? Especially after I worked so hard to improve the interpretation and everything else I got such low marks for at Praterville. After running it through my head over and over all day, I can come up with only two reasons. One, the judges really don't like me because of what I said at Praterville. Or two, Greg's right.

I don't know which option is worse, because I can't figure out how to fix either one.

"And this is my room," Miyu says as she opens the door with a flourish. I peek in to see a room done entirely in her favorite colors—red and yellow. It looks like a McDonald's exploded inside.

"It's . . . red," I say.

"Candy-apple red. I like bold colors."

I sit carefully on the shiny gold bedspread. The doorbell rings, and Miyu runs to answer it. I'm glad I got here first. I knew Mom would want to spend at least a half hour talking to Mrs. Murakami, and I did *not* want to be the girl whose mom hangs around and gossips during the sleepover.

Miyu arrives with two other girls and her arms loaded down with food.

"This is my friend Kaitlin, from skating," Miyu says as she arranges bags of chips and plates of raw veggies. "Kaitlin, this is Sydney and Jane."

"Did you just move here?" the girl with brown hair asks. Sydney, I think.

"No. I—"

"Wait! I remember you from elementary school. Chauncey Elementary." Jane drops an overnight bag on the floor and pounces on the chips. I remember her, too, only about a foot shorter. She's got to be at least five foot seven, and she has this cute, blond bobbed haircut.

"Yeah, I remember you. You had that awesome birthday party at the zoo."

Jane laughs, a loud, infectious laugh. I can't help but laugh with her. "That was a blast, wasn't it?"

"How was the competition this weekend?" Sydney asks as she flops behind me onto Miyu's bed.

"Awful." Miyu frowns. "I couldn't have skated worse."

"Did you go?" Sydney asks me.

I nod. "I have this tango program I can't seem to get." *Or maybe the judges just don't like me,* but I don't say that.

"Figure skating doesn't make any sense," Jane says. "Give me basketball any day. At least it's straightforward. The ball either goes in the basket or it doesn't."

"Maybe we should take up basketball," I say to Miyu as I grab a carrot stick.

She laughs. "Right. A couple of just-over-five-foot-tall basketball players. We'd be great. Besides, no matter how I do, I love skating. When I land a jump, it's the best feeling in the world."

I smile. I know exactly what she means. But I can't get over a lousy placement so easily.

"Where do you go to school, Kaitlin?" Sydney rolls onto her stomach and waits for an answer.

"Um . . . I don't. I do homeschool."

"Lucky," Jane says.

I shrug. "It's not all that fun. There're no clubs or dances or anything. Though it's not like I'd have time to do any of that if I did go to regular school. Because of skating."

"Why not?" Jane asks. "Miyu does academic team. And yearbook."

"And I helped you out with that polar bear swim fund-raiser last year, remember?" Miyu looks up from the backpack she's digging through.

Jane sighs. "You'll never let me forget that, will you?"

"Not a chance. It was freezing!"

It sounds miserable, but I kind of wish I'd been there too. "How do you have time for all of that and skating, too?" I ask Miyu.

She tosses the backpack onto the floor and hauls her skate bag out from her closet. "I make time. That's why I left my old club. They wanted everyone to be all skating, all the time. That just wasn't my thing. I love to skate, and I put everything into it when I'm at the rink, but it's not the only thing I love, you know?"

I remember something Braedon said. "So that's your story?"

Miyu's forehead creases. "My what?"

"Never mind." Somehow I thought her reason for being at Fallton would be way more scandalous, but what she said makes sense. No other really serious coach would put up with a part-time skater.

"What are you looking for in there?" Jane asks through a mouthful of chips. "Please say it's a brown paper bag full of money you found on the way home from school last week."

"Or Mark Benson," Sydney adds.

"Duck, Kaitlin," Jane says.

I slouch down as Jane chucks a carrot stick at Sydney. "You're obsessed with Mark."

"No, I'm not." Sydney smiles. "But he *does* have that swishy hair."

Now that's something I understand.

"Aha!" Miyu stands up with a stack of DVD cases in her hands. "Found them."

"Movies, perfect! What did you get?" Jane asks.

Miyu flips through the cases one by one. "*Strictly Ballroom. Dirty Dancing. Take the Lead. Mad Hot Ballroom.*"

"Wait. Are those all movies about dancing?" Jane's making a face.

"Well, the last one's technically a documentary—"

"I looooove dancing." Sydney jumps up and starts waltzing around the room with one of Miyu's pillows.

Miyu looks at me. "I got these for you. Maybe they'll inspire you."

"I doubt anything will help. It was a nice thought, though." Right now the only way to help my disaster of a program would be to get rid of it.

Miyu hands the movies to Sydney, who picks one and loads it up in Miyu's DVD player. "You can't give up that easily," she says as she sits next to me.

"I'm not giving up. I'm just admitting that I'm not good at tango. I'm a skater, not a dancer." I cross my arms and watch Jane search for the cheesiest chip in the bag.

"You've barely even tried," Miyu says.

"I've taken tango classes, I did a dance lesson with Svetlana, I've listened to Greg. None of it's working."

"Then, who knows, maybe these movies will help. Or I can sign you up to audition for one of those reality dance shows."

I laugh. "Now *that* really would be a disaster."

"You just can't give up, okay? You're too good of a skater for that. Promise?" She holds out her hand and sticks out her pinkie.

I keep my arms crossed.

"I'll just sit here like this all night," Miyu says.

"Fine. Pinkie swear promise," I say, and link my little finger with hers. She's right. Skating is my dream. I can't give up on it just because I had two bad competitions. "Now let's see if any of these movies can teach me how to 'make flirt eyes.'"

Miyu giggles at my awful Svetlana impression. Sydney flips off the lights, and we all crowd together in front of Miyu's bed as the movie starts.

We've finished *Dirty Dancing* and are halfway through *Strictly Ballroom* when there's a knock at Miyu's window.

Chapter Twenty-Four

"What in the world?" Miyu says.

"Do you have a secret boyfriend?" Sydney demands as she hits pause on the movie. "Only secret boyfriends come knock at girls' windows."

"No stupid boy better ever knock on my window," Jane says.

Miyu rolls her eyes. "I do *not* have a secret boyfriend. Or any boyfriend."

"Maybe it's Mark Benson," I say, remembering how Sydney was sort of cooing over him earlier.

"Ooh! Go look." Sydney pulls Miyu up from the floor. Miyu

takes the whole three steps to her window and raises the blinds.

"Seriously?" she says. "Why are you here?"

"Is it Mark?" Sydney crowds over Miyu's shoulder. "That's not Mark. Who is that? He's cute."

Jane looks at me. I shrug. Together we get up and see who the mystery guy at Miyu's window is. I stand on my tiptoes to peek over Miyu's other shoulder.

Braedon's leaning against the big oak tree just outside the window. "Are you guys playing Truth or Dare? I pick dare. What do I have to do? Eat six jalapeño peppers? Prank call someone?"

Miyu just shakes her head. I'm pretty sure she's rolling her eyes, too, even though I can't see her face.

Sydney elbows me. "Where did he come from?" she whispers.

"*He* came from the rink. And now he'd better go home." Miyu starts to pull her window down.

Braedon leaps forward. "Wait a second. I'm here to talk to Kaitlin."

He came to see me? I kind of wish I hadn't eaten those carrots. They feel like they're tangoing in my stomach right now.

"Do you need me to punch him?" Jane asks me.

I shake my head.

"She has a phone. You can call her," Miyu says out the window.

"Miyu!" Sydney pushes her a little sideways. "Hey there," she says to Braedon with a smile. "Kaitlin's here." She grabs my arm and pulls me into Miyu's spot.

"Just tell him to go away," Miyu says before she moves back to stand with Jane.

"Hey, Double Axel." Braedon pushes his hair out of his eyes.

Sydney sighs. I totally get it. He makes me want to sigh too.

"Hi," is all I say.

He smiles at me. "Can I come in?"

I open my mouth, but Miyu speaks first. "No! This is my room. You can't barge in like it's some random locker room at the rink."

Braedon laughs a little. "Well, then, can you come outside?" he asks me.

"Um . . ."

"She's hanging out with us, and she's not into sneaking out," Miyu says from behind me.

Sydney reaches back to swat at Miyu, while I stare at Braedon and try to form words.

"Kaitlin?" Braedon shoves his hands into his pockets.

"Um . . . sure." I glance back at Miyu, who looks like her eyes are about to pop out of her head. "Just for a few minutes."

Sydney practically squeals with excitement as she helps me push up the screen and climb through the window. My feet dangle for a second before I drop to the ground.

I can't believe I'm doing this. I just climbed out of a window to see a guy. Miyu's frowning at me from the window. Mom would completely lose it if she found out.

What's wrong with me?

But it's not like I'm running off somewhere with him. I just came outside to talk for a few minutes. That's not so bad, right?

"Come *on*, Syd. Give them some privacy already." Jane pulls a grinning Sydney away from the window.

"Just knock when you're ready to come back in," Miyu says as she pulls the screen back into place. "But if you're not back in fifteen minutes, I'm coming out there." With that, she thumps the window down and disappears into her room.

I follow Braedon around the other side of the tree. The sun is starting to set across the street, and the light makes his face look orange. Which means it's probably making my face orange too. I turn my head toward the tree to try to cut down on the Oompa Loompa look.

"I'm going to Burger Hut. You want to come?" he asks.

Yes! I want to yell. But instead I cross my arms and glance back at Miyu's window. "I would, but I'm at this sleepover. . . ."

Braedon shrugs. "They'll still be here when you get back."

True, but it seems super rude to take off with Braedon when I'm supposed to be hanging out with Miyu and her friends. And then there's the whole sneaking out thing.

"Sorry . . . I should stay here. We have food inside."

"Rabbit food, I bet," he says. "A big plate full of lettuce, carrots, celery, raw broccoli. Yum." He rubs a hand over his stomach.

I laugh. "How'd you guess? But we have chips, too."

"You know you'd rather have a big, greasy burger and fries." He stretches an arm out to prop himself against the tree.

"Maybe another time?" As soon as I say it, I can't believe it came out of my mouth. I'm making a date with Braedon.

"Okay." He doesn't say anything about when.

"Okay," I repeat. "See you at the rink. I should . . . um . . . get back inside." I motion at the window.

Braedon walks with me around the tree. "Thanks for braving the wrath of Miyu to come out and talk to me."

I smile as I knock on the window. "Anytime."

He disappears as Miyu lifts the glass and the screen. I find a brick that sticks out a little more than the others on the side of Miyu's house and use it to hoist myself back inside.

Once I'm in, Sydney peppers me with questions. "Who is that? Is he your boyfriend? Where does he go to school? How'd you meet him? How does he get his hair to look like that?"

Even Jane, who was ready to punch him in the nose, looks interested. It's fun, sharing this stuff. And it's nice not talking about skating all the time.

This is what it would be like if I went to school.

"Sorry," I say to Miyu when Sydney starts the movie again. "I know you don't like him."

"I don't care about him," Miyu says. "It's you I'm worried about."

That makes zero sense. "There's nothing to worry about. I'm okay."

As the movie rolls on, I'm only paying half attention to it. I'm wondering if Miyu's being worried about me has something to do with what she said back at Pizza Supreme—that Braedon isn't serious about skating or anything.

But as hard as I think, I can't figure out how him not caring about his skating or his grades in school has anything to do with me.

———·····———

While I'm warming up on the ice Tuesday morning, Braedon joins me. "How was the sleepover?" he asks.

"Fun." I do a quick turn so I'm skating backward. "Did you get your burger and fries?"

"No, didn't want to go by myself. So that means you owe me a trip to Burger Hut. Maybe later this week?"

"Um, sure." I shiver—and not from the cold of the rink. I pull up to the boards for a sip of water, since my throat is suddenly dry.

Addison skids to a stop next to us. "Hey, I want to show you something," she says to Braedon.

"Double axel?" he asks. "Did you land it?"

"Maybe." She smirks at me. "You'd better practice, Kaitlin. Fourteenth place won't get you to Nationals." She grabs Braedon's arm. "Come on."

And off they go, leaving me alone at the boards. Something sour rises into my throat. I definitely don't feel sorry for Addison anymore. I don't know what to think about Braedon. I thought he liked me, but maybe he just wants someone to eat burgers with.

Greg glides over while I'm watching Addison attempt double axels for Braedon. "Ready to work that program again?" he asks.

"I guess." I pull my eyes away from Addison and Braedon and try to focus on Greg.

"I know you're disappointed about the competition."

"I thought I'd skated better than that," I say.

"Your elements were perfect. It was your disconnect from the music that landed you in fourteenth place."

"What if . . ." I don't know. It feels like whining to ask Greg if the real reason might be my outburst at Praterville.

Greg raises an eyebrow. "What if what?"

I stab at the ice with my toe pick. "What if it's because the judges don't like me? Because of what I said to them? I know it's not the same judges, but I'm sure they talk to each other."

Greg sighs. "Well, you didn't make it any easier for yourself with that reaction. But you sent apology letters, right?"

I nod.

"Then you've done all you can to fix that mistake. Now you have to focus on the future. If you wow them—if you skate a program that gets to their souls—they can't help but give you the scores you deserve. But you have to work for it. Are you willing to work for it?"

"Yes. Definitely. I want to go to Nationals more than anything. But I tried in Chicago, and I couldn't do it. The emotional thing, I mean."

"It's in there." Greg taps his chest. "You just have to find a way to bring what's inside to the outside. Pull it out and let it work through you, to every part of your body, even your fingertips."

He starts the music, and I try to tango with my fingertips. Addison's mom is in her usual spot on the bleachers, watching her daughter's every move. I pretend she's a judge. How do I make her feel my program in her soul? How did Baby show everyone the way she felt in that last dance in *Dirty Dancing*?

When the music ends, Greg shakes his head. "You've got the technical skills. We just need to make you a dancer. And we've got about three weeks to do it."

"I'm doing the tango classes, but I usually end up dancing with Addison. And I took that ice dance lesson, like you said," I tell him.

"Hmm. Maybe if you skated with a partner. An actual partner, not Addison." Greg scans the rink. "Wait here a second."

He glides to the boards, where Tom is chatting with Samantha. They talk for a second, and then Greg returns with Tom behind him.

Oh no. What is he going to make me do now? Whatever it is, it can't possibly be as bad as forced flirting with Braedon.

But at least Braedon is almost the same age as me. Tom has to be at least fifteen.

But I have to try. I promised Miyu. And I want Nationals so badly. If I don't keep trying, then there's no way I'll do any better at Regionals than I have at any other competitions lately. I guess this is what Greg meant when he said he thought the judges were pushing me. Maybe he's right. It's not like I insulted them *before* the Praterville competition. And I never got such low scores last year. At least I hope he's right. . . .

"You've learned the Canasta Tango, right?" Greg asks.

I nod. It's the second easiest dance—one that I'd learned a long time ago, and that Svetlana had me go through the week before the Chicago competition.

"Good. You're going to skate it with Tom. Take your cues from him."

What does that mean? Tom grabs my hands and puts them in the right place. I'm glad I have gloves on, because my palms are all sweaty.

"Ready?" he asks. "Greg wants me to help you with your tango expression."

The music starts, and he's almost dragging me along with him. I've never skated so fast in my life.

"You've got to look at me, not your feet," he says over the music.

I can't help looking at my feet. I'm scared to death that I'll trip over my toe picks or kick him in the shin. But I have to do it or Greg will just make me dance with him again. Plus, maybe it will actually help my program. I drag my eyes up to Tom's face—and crack up.

Tom is looking at me with the most intense expression I've ever seen in my life.

"Kaitlin, you can't laugh," he says, letting a little smile break through his Serious Tango Face. "Tango is all smoldering glances and passion."

"I *know*," I say. "Greg's only told me that five hundred times."

"I know it's weird, but you can do it if you take it seriously," he says.

I try to smolder.

"You look like you've just eaten rotten fish," Tom says.

"Thanks. How does Samantha do this without laughing?"

"We've been skating together since we were nine years old. We're sort of used to each other now." Tom says all this while keeping that crazy intense expression on his face. "Use your eyes more," he says.

How do I do that? My eyes are attached in my head. It's not like I can wave them around or something. And what is it with ice dancers and eyes? Svetlana was all about the eyes too.

"That's better," he says.

I wish I knew what I'd done to make it better.

The music stops. I'm completely out of breath from skating so fast and trying to smolder and use my eyes.

"I think you got it toward the end, Kaitlin," Greg says. "Now use that in your program."

Tom returns to Samantha, and I skate my program again. I pretend I'm skating with Tom. I smolder while I count the steps in my footwork. I use my eyes. I try to look like I haven't eaten rotten fish. I do it all while I think through my program piece by piece. The music ends, and I turn toward Greg.

He shakes his head.

I'm never going to get this.

Chapter Twenty-Five

Mom leans out the window of the car. "Are you sure you'll be okay by yourself?"

"Mom, yes! It's just a dance class." And I'm actually a little excited that she's just dropping me off. I mean, she rarely watches every move I make on the ice, but she's always there. Like she's babysitting me or something.

"Okay. Call if you need me. I'll be back in an hour." Mom waves as she backs out of her parking spot and heads to the grocery store.

"Hey, Double Axel!" a guy's voice calls from down the sidewalk just as I'm about to push the studio door open.

"Braedon?" A wave of warmth rushes through me as I let the door go and step back. There he is, headed right toward me. "What are you doing here? Did you sign up for dance class too?"

"No way." He stops in front of me and pushes his hair out of his eyes. My heart beats just a little faster. "Besides, I have a better idea. Skip and come to Burger Hut with me," Braedon says.

I peek inside the glass door of the studio. Fernando's there, gliding across the shiny wooden floor with one of the giggling older ladies. Almost everyone's already inside, ready for the class to start. "I don't know . . . I really have to work on my expression."

"But you owe me a burger, remember?" Braedon smiles at me.

Would it really be so awful if I missed one class? I've been to a bunch so far, and there are still a few more before Regionals.

I know I shouldn't, though. I still haven't nailed whatever it is that Greg thinks I need to make this program work. And if we got caught, Mom would ground me for all eternity. I could hang up any chance of Dad convincing her to let me go to school.

But Braedon came all the way over here, from . . . somewhere. He wasn't at the rink this afternoon, and he's still wearing his St. Benedict's uniform. And he's giving me that adorable grin. I feel a little melty, like the ice on a ninety-degree afternoon.

"Okay."

"Really?" Braedon's face lights up.

Just then the door opens. Addison steps out, looking perfect in tight black pants, a black top, and a little red tie-on skirt. "What are you doing out here?" she asks me. Then she notices Braedon, and her frown dissolves. "Hi, Braedon."

"Hey," he says. "Double Axel and I are going to Burger Hut. You want to come?"

Is he seriously inviting Addison? My face goes red. Maybe this isn't a date after all. Maybe we are just friends.

Addison gives him a flirty smile and twists her ponytail with her finger. "I'd love to, but Kaitlin and I have tango class right now. Come on, K, it's about to start."

K? Since when does Addison call me by a nickname?

"Um, I'm kind of hungry. I'm going to the Burger Hut instead," I say.

Addison's fake friendly smile retreats into her usual frown.

"You're skipping class? Can you really afford to do that with Regionals coming up?"

"One class won't make or break her chances at qualifying," Braedon says. "Not with that double axel."

Addison looks like he just punched her in the stomach. She hasn't even landed a double axel, as far as I know. "Fine," she says as Mrs. Thomas taps impatiently on the studio window. Addison nods at her mom, and then turns back to me. "So where's your mother, Kaitlin?"

There's something about the way she narrows her eyes at me. I know she's not just asking where Mom is. It's almost like a threat. As in, *You go off with Braedon, and I'm so telling your mother you skipped class.*

I swallow hard. "At the grocery store. She'll be here later."

"Hmm." Addison gives me a little smirk, and then disappears back inside.

"What was that all about?" Braedon asks.

"I think she's going to rat me out." Now I'm not sure I should go. Is this worth getting into loads of trouble with Mom?

Braedon pulls on his loosened St. Benedict's tie. "She wouldn't do that."

"I don't know. . . ."

"You're not going to stand me up again, are you?" He gives

me this sad puppy-dog look. "We'll eat fast and have plenty of time to get back before your mom. If Addison does say anything, you can deny it all."

That is true. There's no way Mom would believe Addison over me.

"Okay, let's go." I take a step forward and stop. "Wait, how are we getting there? Did you steal a car?"

He laughs, and for a split second, I wonder if he did. It seems like the kind of thing he'd find fun.

"No, we have to walk. Sorry. But it's not very far."

It isn't, but there aren't any sidewalks here either. Just a really busy street and some overgrown grass between the parking lots of stores and gas stations.

Mom got me a pair of black heels called character shoes. They aren't very high ones, of course, and I can only wear them for dance. The heels are sinking into the soft ground between a Gas Up station and a Good Times Family Buffet. "Ugh . . . mud!"

Braedon laughs as I rub my shoe against the grass. It doesn't do a lot of good, though. The black heel is now brown. I'll have to clean them off before Mom sees. "So gross."

"Burger Hut is worth it. Just think of having a good, greasy burger instead of your usual rabbit food."

"I don't just eat rabbit food," I say, but he's already scrambling up a small hill toward the Burger Hut parking lot.

"So, where were you today? I didn't see you at the rink," I ask Braedon after we get our food and sit in a booth in the back. Just the two of us.

I'm still not sure if this counts as a date. I mean, he came just to get me, but then he invited Addison, too. But if it *is* a date . . . The whole idea makes me want to smile and throw up at the same time.

"Didn't feel like skating. Ended up hanging out with a couple of guys from school instead." He squirts ketchup from one of those little plastic packets onto the open wrapper of his burger.

"Won't your parents be mad that you skipped practice?"

"Probably."

He doesn't seem to want to talk about it, so I change the subject. "Are you nervous about Regionals?"

"Not really," he says through a mouthful of food. "I never qualify for Nationals, so it's just another competition for me."

"Don't you want to?"

"Sure, I guess. Doesn't everyone? But it'll never happen. And even if it did, I would have to practice more and work harder. That's no fun." He pushes his hair out of his eyes and takes another bite of burger.

I don't know what to say to that. Miyu just skates for fun, but even she wants to qualify for Nationals. And somehow I know that if she did, she'd take it seriously and work as hard as she could to do well. "So why do you skate?" I finally ask Braedon.

He drags some fries through the pool of ketchup. "I don't know. Because I always have? I like jumping."

"Me too. It's like flying for a second, and when I land a jump, I feel so good. Like I've done something really incredible. Like I've done something no one else can do."

"Yeah, just like that. If all I had to do was go out there and jump, it would be great. No spins or footwork or artistic interpretation."

I roll my eyes. "Don't get me started on artistic interpretation."

"Still can't flirt, huh?"

My cheeks heat up and I concentrate on rescuing the lettuce and tomato sliding out of my bun. "You really don't like to spin?" I ask, hoping he won't bring up the flirting thing again.

"Not really. I mean, it's okay, but I don't get the same thrill from it as jumping. Give me a good triple salchow over a perfect camel any day."

"I wish I had a triple sal," I say. "Then the judges would have to notice me, whether I can tango or not."

"They notice you. It's kind of hard to forget the girl who spoke her mind and then took out the medals table."

I put my burger down. That's all I'm ever going to be. The skater who lost her composure and ruined her whole career.

"Hey, Double Axel? I meant that as a compliment." Braedon's giving me this concerned look.

"Thanks? I don't know if it's doing much to help Fallton's reputation, though."

Braedon waves a fry at me. "You couldn't do anything to change that—good or bad."

"It's not fair, though. We have really good skaters, but everyone writes us off."

"I know. But why worry about something you can't control?"

"I guess." I chew my last bite of burger and wish there was something we could do.

Chapter Twenty-Six

Braedon walks me back to the dance studio, and I slip inside with ten minutes to spare. Jill gives me a funny look but keeps moving around the room, checking arm position here and demonstrating steps there. Up front, Addison's dancing with Fernando. Her mom is beaming, like Addison's going to get the award for World's Best Tango Dancer.

When the class ends, I move toward the door to wait for Mom.

"I hope it was worth it," Addison says over my shoulder.

"Worth what?"

She glances back at her mother, who's talking with

Fernando. "My mom didn't see you leave. But if I told her, she'd probably say something to your mom. You won't get to eat burgers with Braedon if you're grounded, you know."

I bite my lip. Maybe it wasn't such a good idea. It definitely sounds like Addison is going to tell her mother. What if Mom believes what Mrs. Thomas says? Not only will I be grounded, she'll never trust me to be alone anywhere, including school.

Mom pulls up outside. Without a word to Addison, I sprint out the door and jump in the car.

"How was class?" Mom asks.

"Great." I'm watching the dance studio disappear in the side mirror.

Addison's probably already talking to her mother. I am so dead.

As the Zamboni plods across the ice on Saturday morning, I search for Braedon in the crowded lobby. I spot him leaning against the concrete block wall next to the snack bar, drinking water and watching the Zam move in slow circles. After I make sure Mom is busy talking with some of the other parents—and that Addison and her mom aren't here yet—I move toward Braedon.

"Hey, Double Axel, long time no see," he says.

My stomach jumps at his lazy smile. Then I remember the world of trouble I'm going to be in once Addison gets here.

"So . . . um, that was fun last night. The burgers, I mean. But I kind of can't do anything like that again," I say.

Braedon sets his water on the snack bar counter. "Why not?"

"Because Addison's going to tell her mom, who will definitely say something to my mom."

"I told you, she wouldn't do anything like that."

"She pretty much told me that she was." I roll up to the tips of my blade guards and search the lobby—just in time to see Addison and Mrs. Thomas walk in.

"I'll talk to her." Braedon grabs his water bottle and strides across the lobby to meet Addison.

"It's probably too late," I say to his back.

I stay put near the snack bar, watching. I can't hear them from here, but Braedon's smiling and Addison looks really annoyed. She glances up at me and glares. I bite my lip and cross my fingers. Maybe she hasn't said anything yet.

Then he must say something funny, because she laughs. He claps her once on the back before heading back toward me. She watches him, all happy and smug-looking, and then turns toward her mother.

"What did she say?" I ask the second he gets close enough to hear me.

"She didn't tell her mom yet. She promised to keep it quiet." He pushes his hair out of his eyes, looking pleased with himself.

"How did you make that happen?" I can't imagine what he would've said to convince Addison not to get me in heaps of trouble.

He taps his gloved fingertips together like some old movie villain. "I have my ways."

He looks so silly that I can't help laughing. "Thanks," I say.

"No problem. Hey, look, the Zam's done." And with that, Braedon tosses his water bottle into the air, catches it, and walks off toward the ice. Near the doors, Addison catches up with him. She says something, and he touches her arm and laughs.

My happy feeling floats away. I wonder what exactly it was that Braedon told Addison to change her mind.

When I'm not in my lesson, I spend most of the two back-to-back skating sessions watching Braedon help Addison with her double axel and worrying about whether she'll really keep my huge mistake a secret. And about whether I missed the one thing in tango class that could've made my program perfect.

I don't get a chance to talk to Miyu until after the last skating session. I sit next to her while we wait for Karilee's Movement and Interpretation class to begin.

"Are you mad at me?" I ask her quietly. I'd told her on the phone last night about going to Burger Hut with Braedon.

She sighs. "No. I'm just confused, I guess." Miyu unties and reties her shoelace. "You want to win Regionals, and now you're skipping out on a class you're taking to do that, just to hang out with Braedon?"

"I know. It was kind of a dumb thing to do."

"But you still have a crush on Braedon."

"I don't have a crush on him!" I hiss at her.

"Yes, you do. It's so obvious, Kaitlin. All he does is look at you, and you turn all red and giggle."

"I don't giggle!"

Miyu gives me a look.

"Okay . . . maybe I like him a little. But I don't giggle. I don't know if it even matters. He seems to be into Addison, anyway."

Miyu shrugs. "Who knows? Just remember what I said about him before. I mean, he's been expelled from how many schools? And he's definitely not serious about skating."

"You're not serious about skating," I say defensively, even though I know exactly what she means.

"I am, just in a different way than you are. If Braedon's mom didn't make him come to the rink, I doubt he'd skate at all."

What was it Braedon said at Burger Hut yesterday? He skates because he always has. Not being ultracompetitive about skating hardly makes him a bad person. But then there's the whole skipping practice sessions and getting me to leave my dance class thing. Kind of red flags.

What I *should* do is forget about Braedon. At least until after Regionals.

But I don't know if I can.

Chapter Twenty-Seven

Greg keeps me busy all week running my program, sending me off to more ice dance time with Svetlana, and telling me to feel my music. No matter how many times he says that, it still doesn't seem to be working.

At least Addison's kept her word to Braedon. Neither she nor her mom has said anything about me not being at dance class last week.

"Ah, Kaitlin!" Jill swoops in as Mom grabs a seat at the far end of the row from Mrs. Thomas. "Glad to see you here on time this week."

Mom tilts her head, and I can tell she's about to say something to Jill. Something like, *You must have my daughter confused with someone else. Kaitlin was five minutes early last week.*

"I have a question about the *ochos*," I say to Jill as I step away from Mom. "Is it like this?" I do some completely wrong thing with my feet on purpose.

"No, no, no. Like this." Jill demonstrates. I look over her shoulder to see Mom pecking away at her phone.

"Thanks. I've got it, I think."

"You know, you miss a lot when you're not in class," Jill says.

"I know. I'm sorry." I glance past Jill to make sure Mom's not listening in. "I just got caught up in something last week." Something like eating fries with Braedon. "I won't miss any more classes."

Jill nods, and I hope I've said enough so that she won't bring it up with Mom. I'm already barely hanging on with the Praterville thing and being late to stretching class that one day. I'd never have a life again if she found out about me missing dance. But sometimes I feel as if the secret is like a rat, gnawing at me from the inside out.

On top of all that, Regionals is only two weeks away, and Greg insists I'm still not showing enough emotion in my program.

———·····———

At least the club's Regionals send-off party is something I don't have to worry about. Greg told me they have the party early so no one will get distracted during the nine days we have left. I sip a cup of punch and survey everyone hanging out in the Fallton lobby. Mom and Dad are mingling with some of the other parents near the snack bar under a huge sign that reads GOOD LUCK AT REGIONALS! I left Miyu, Addison, and a couple of other girls sitting on chairs and talking. Well, Addison wasn't actually talking, just scowling at everyone.

I take my punch to the rink doors and push through them. The music from the party is pounding, even out here. The ice is shiny and wet, with fresh, mountain-size bumps in nice straight lines. I close my eyes and breathe in the cold and quiet and the slight hint of ammonia and Zamboni fumes. Ice rinks smell the same, no matter how big or small or where they are.

"Imagining yourself finally landing that triple sal?" Braedon's voice interrupts my thoughts.

I almost drop my punch. "I didn't think anyone was out here," I say. "By the way, congrats on your award."

Braedon holds up a certificate. "The Dennis the Menace Award? I think I'd rather have yours."

I grin at him. "They gave me Best Jumper for a reason, you know."

Braedon pushes his hair out of his eyes. "Yeah, I guess I should at least be happy they didn't give me Nicest Skater or Best Personality." He puts his certificate on the nearest bleacher. "Hey, you want to see something cool?"

"Sure, I guess." I set my punch cup next to his certificate and follow him across the mats between the ice and the bleachers. "So, um, thanks for talking to Addison."

"Anytime," he says as he leads the way around to where the boards branch out from the ice and create a short wall between the bleachers area and where the Zamboni enters and leaves the ice.

"There won't be any other time. I can't do that again, remember?"

Braedon doesn't answer. Instead he hops up onto the wall and slides over to the other side. "C'mon."

I rest my arms on the wall. "Are we supposed to be back there?"

"Not really," he says with a grin. Then he holds out his hand. "Here, I'll help you."

My brain is screaming, *No way!* I glance back toward the lobby. The windows face the ice. If anyone was watching us, they'd have to smoosh their faces sideways against the Plexiglas to see.

But isn't this just like skipping dance class or climbing out Miyu's window? Maybe it isn't, though. I mean, we aren't supposed to be here, but it isn't like we're really doing anything bad.

"Kaitlin, are you coming?" Braedon wiggles his fingers. His hair falls into his face again, and I can't help but smile.

Ignoring the voice in my head telling me this is stupid, I climb up on the wall. I take his hand, which makes my heart beat even faster. Thank God ice rinks are cold. Otherwise, my hand would be all hot and sweaty and embarrassing. Braedon helps me hop off the other side of the wall. There aren't any rubber mats on the floor here—just concrete and wet, melty ice.

The door to the garage that houses the Zamboni is wide open. The machine sits inside, rusty and huge and dripping condensation.

"Ever sat on a Zam before?" Braedon asks.

I shake my head. He walks over to it and hoists himself up into the driver's seat.

"Come on up. The view's great!"

I laugh. It looks like fun, but I know we shouldn't even be near this thing. I can't even imagine how Mom would freak out if she caught me. Or how Greg would react. And another thought crosses my mind—is sitting on a Zamboni reason enough to kick someone out of a skating club?

"What are you waiting for?" Braedon asks. "No one's going to see us. Even if they came out, they couldn't see us way back here. We'd have plenty of time to get down and back over the wall."

I glance again toward the lobby. Everyone's still inside. When I turn around, Braedon's pushed his hair back and is looking at me with those bright blue eyes. I grab his hand and make the climb. Once I'm up there, I have to squeeze past him. There's no passenger seat—just a ledge with a bunch of levers and things I try not to touch. I step up onto the ledge and perch on a big, rusty-looking, gray cylinder. My knees are about even with the top of Braedon's head.

I gaze over the hood. "Wow, this would be a great place to watch a competition. You can see the entire ice. Wouldn't it be great if Regionals were here instead of in Indianapolis?" I imagine myself doing my program out there, on comfortable ice—home ice. The competition would somehow seem less scary if it happened here.

"I don't think anyone would be nicer just because they had to compete here. That would probably make it even worse," Braedon says.

I clench my hands. "We work just as hard as everyone else. Why is it okay for them to make fun of us because of our club?"

Braedon puts his hands on the steering wheel, like he's about to drive the machine onto the ice. "I don't know. Nothing we can do about it, so no reason to worry. I wonder what this thing does." He spins a knob that's sticking out of the front of the steering wheel.

"But aren't you sick of it? Working so hard, doing well in competition—sometimes—and still having people call us the Fall Down Club?"

He shrugs. It doesn't bother him, I guess. I wonder if he'd be happier if he quit.

"I just wish there was something we could do to change it." I cross my ankles and bump my sneaker heels against the cylinder.

"What, like put up posters protesting mean skaters? Or you could make them all bracelets. Or wait—we could put 'nice' medicine into everyone's bottled water." Braedon laughs at his own joke while the music from the party thumps through the empty rink, making the Plexiglas on top of the dasher boards shiver.

"No . . . wait." I sit up so straight I almost slide right off the cylinder. I grip the sides for balance. "That's it!"

"What? The bottled water? I'm all for a good prank, but that's a little off the deep end, Double Axel."

"Not that. Not the posters, either, but . . . what if we did something nice for everyone? Something that made them all realize that we're just normal, regular skaters. And that we're really fun and friendly. Just something that makes them think twice before they say mean stuff or cut holes in our practice clothes, you know?"

"But how?" Braedon reaches past my foot and plays with the shifter-looking thing near his knee, making noises like he's driving the machine.

"That's the problem. I don't know. I doubt beaded bracelets will cut it."

"No way . . . look! Someone left the keys." Braedon turns the ignition to the Zam, but it doesn't start.

"Maybe we should go back in." I stand up, ready to hop off the ledge, when Braedon pushes a button near the steering wheel and the Zamboni roars to life.

Then it begins to creep forward.

I sway and grab hold of the cold metal cylinder. "What did you do? Make it stop!"

"I don't know. I didn't think that button would do anything.

There's got to be a brake down here somewhere." Braedon peers past his legs at the floor.

We're rolling out of the garage at the speed of a turtle, but kind of at an angle, like the steering wheel is turned.

"Hit the brake! We're going to run into the wall." I can't let go of the cylinder. I'm gripping it so hard, my knuckles turn white.

"I'm trying. I don't know where the brakes are." Braedon pushes on one pedal. The engine revs. It's so loud, it might drown out the music at the party.

My hands are definitely hot and sweaty now. I can't take my eyes off the wall coming closer and closer. "Try another pedal."

"I don't see another one."

"Then look harder!"

"Maybe it's one of these lever things." Braedon pushes and pulls on the levers sticking up from the ledge. The one closest to his knee just seems to make the Zamboni move faster. He pulls on one behind him, and the big machine makes a horrible grinding noise from underneath us. But it's still lumbering toward the wall. "Why won't this thing stop?"

"Wait, push that button again." I point to it and feel sort of sick that I didn't think of it before.

But it's too late. I watch in horror as the front driver's side of the Zam collides with the short white wall.

Chapter Twenty-Eight

There's a shattering sound, like glass breaking, and then scraping, and the machine finally stops.

Braedon's eyes are huge as he peers over the side of the Zam. I'm frozen to my seat. We stare at the doors to the lobby, waiting for everyone to come running out.

Nothing happens. The music thumps from the party, so loud it must've covered up the chugging of the Zamboni and the sickening sound of it hitting the wall.

Braedon turns to me. "Get out! We have to get out of here before someone catches us." His hand shakes as he punches the button and turns the ignition off.

I make my legs move and jump to the ground after Braedon. I can't help but look at the Zam as we pass the smashed corner to crawl back over the wall. The headlight is broken and the front corner is dented in. Part of it still rests against the wall, and I'm sure it's completely scraped up.

"Let's go, Kaitlin! The sooner we get back, the better." He pulls me over and we hurry past the rows of bleachers to the lobby doors. Braedon peeks through the windows.

"Wait! Our stuff." I run back to the first row of bleachers.

My cup and Braedon's certificate are gone. I scan all the bleachers, but they're nowhere to be found.

"Who cares? It's just a stupid fake award. Let's get inside." Braedon pushes one of the doors open.

I race over to slip in with him. "Someone must have come out and picked them up. They're going to know it was us out there!"

"They can't prove anything," Braedon whispers.

I follow him to where Miyu, Samantha, and Addison are standing, drinking their punch, surrounded by clumps of people talking and having fun.

"What's wrong, Kaitlin? You look like you've seen a ghost." Miyu tilts her head as she studies my face.

"She's nervous about Regionals, of course," Addison says. "I'm not."

“I’m fine,” I say to Miyu. “Just . . . like Addison says, nervous.”

Miyu raises her eyebrows. I’m paranoid she doesn’t believe me. “You need to de-stress,” she says. “We’ve got over a week till Regionals.”

Addison takes a big gulp of punch from her cup. “This is really good. Didn’t you have some earlier, Kaitlin?”

I glance at her. “Um . . . yeah. It was okay.”

Addison gives me a half smile.

And I know. I know she saw us and she knows exactly what happened.

But before I can say anything to her, Greg claps his hands to get everyone’s attention. “Time for our official send-off! We have goodie bags for all of our Regional competitors.” He starts announcing names, and we go up one by one as everyone claps.

“Hey, look, extra gloves.” Braedon pulls a black pair from his bag.

New gloves are the last thing I can think about. “What if they figure out we were in the Zam?” I whisper to him.

“Relax and stop thinking about it. No one saw us.”

“Addison knows. She asked me about the punch!”

“That doesn’t mean anything. You have to stop talking about it.” Braedon looks around. “We weren’t there and we didn’t do anything.” He strolls off to talk to Tom.

"We?" But I'm talking to myself. I didn't drive the Zam into the wall; he did. But I was there, sitting where I wasn't supposed to be and probably breaking a hundred club rules.

Probably more than enough to get me kicked out.

"We have a serious problem," Greg announces early Thursday morning. "Sometime between last night and this morning, someone started the Zamboni and ran it into the boards."

Chatter rises up across the room. Greg holds up his hand for silence. I look around for Braedon, but he's not here yet. I sit on my hands because I'm sure they're shaking like crazy.

Across the room, I catch Addison's eye. She smiles at me as she twists a lock of hair in her ponytail.

"This means the ice can't be resurfaced," Greg continues. "They expect the machine to be fixed for tomorrow—good enough to cut the ice, at least. Our morning sessions should be fine, but the club will refund the cost of sessions to anyone who decides not to skate this afternoon. Practice the rest of the week should go on as planned. But the problem is more serious than that. I'm sure you all know how expensive a Zamboni is. It costs almost as much as a small house. And the price for repairing one isn't exactly cheap either."

I gulp. Why did I go along with Braedon? I should've said

no, should've gone back to the lobby. What is wrong with me?

And he's not even here. I'm still fuming over how he walked off from me last night. I thought he was my friend. Maybe more than a friend. But he's not. The realization hurts even more than the time I tripped on backward crossovers and plowed into the boards headfirst. I won't make the mistake of hanging out with him again.

"The manager says there was no sign of a break-in," Greg continues. "And our club members were the only ones here last night. Of course, I told the manager that there was no way any of my skaters would do something like that. We respect the rink and its property." His eyes move slowly across the room. "I don't want to be wrong. That's all."

I let out the breath I was holding. Half of me expected Addison to jump in and accuse me. I wish I could tell someone, to get it off my chest. Adding this mess to my stash of secrets and worrying about Regionals is making me jumpy. I glance at Miyu. Maybe I'll tell her. And hope she still wants to be my friend.

Addison corners me on the ice as I'm arranging my stuff on top of the boards. She places her silver water bottle next to my purple plastic one. "So," she says. "What are you going to do?"

I put my package of tissues on top of my CD so I don't have to look at her. "Do about what?"

"Oh, come on, K. I know it was you and Braedon. I have that cup with your name on it and his award. So, what are you going to do?"

I take a deep breath to try to steady my heart rate. "I don't know."

"I have an idea, if you want to hear it." She glances out over the ice as if my answer doesn't interest her at all.

"I don't think I have a choice."

She turns back to me and smiles. "It's not such a big deal. Just stay away from Braedon. If you do that, I'll keep your little secret."

"Girls, practice has started. Less talk, more skate," Greg says as he moves past us.

"Think about it." Addison tightens her ponytail and glides off.

I clench my hands so hard that my nails are digging into my palms, even through my gloves. Staying away from Braedon isn't the issue. I don't want anything to do with him anyway.

The problem is letting Addison win.

Chapter Twenty-Nine

A couple of days pass, and I keep the secret. No one says anything else about the Zamboni, but I feel guilty each time I see Greg. Which is every day.

Braedon. I wouldn't be in this mess if it wasn't for him. He seems to have forgotten about the whole thing. He's laughing and acting completely normal. Not that I'm talking to him at all. Addison probably thinks I've agreed to stay away from him, even though I haven't.

But every time I start to blame Braedon, I hear that little voice in my head reminding me that it was my choice to go along with him.

"What's wrong?" Miyu asks as we wait for Karilee and her boom box to show up for off-ice class on Saturday. "You've been acting really weird ever since the party."

I shrug. "Just nervous, I guess."

Miyu scoots across the floor so that she's sitting right in front of me. "That's not it. I can tell. So what's going on with you and Braedon?" she asks, like that's a better topic to talk about. "You guys were practically inseparable, but I haven't seen you even look at each other since the party. I thought you really liked him."

Luckily, the noise level in the lobby is so high that no one could've heard what Miyu just said. Because I'd die of embarrassment if anyone knew how I felt about Braedon. Or used to feel about him, that is.

Miyu's just sitting there, legs crossed, looking genuinely concerned about my relationship with Braedon. The guy who's pretty much ruined my life. Suddenly I have to tell *someone* about the Zamboni. I cross my fingers and hope she'll still be my friend once she knows.

"Promise you won't tell anyone?"

She scoots closer. "What are you talking about?"

"Just promise?"

"Sure. What happened?"

I take a deep breath and twist my hands together. "You know how someone crashed the Zam at the send-off party?"

"It was Braedon," Miyu says.

I stare at her. "How do you know?"

"No one else would be stupid enough to do that. I figured it had to be him."

I wait until Samantha's walked past us before I talk. "But why didn't you say anything to Greg?"

"I didn't know for sure. I can't just go blaming someone. But it was him, wasn't it?" Miyu slides the locket on her necklace back and forth as she waits for my answer.

"Yeah. It was. But I was sitting next to him." I shut my eyes and relive that moment. My crush on Braedon disappeared the second the Zamboni hit the wall. "You were right. I can't believe I went along with him on all those stupid things. Being late to off-ice, leaving your sleepover, skipping dance, and now crashing the Zam. If anyone finds out, I'll get kicked out of the club."

Miyu shakes her head. "No, you won't. Because you didn't do anything. Yeah, you shouldn't have been sitting on the Zam, but you didn't run it into the wall. Braedon's the one who'll be in trouble."

"Do you think I should tell? What if they kick *him* out?"

"I don't know. But they won't make him leave. Greg wouldn't do something like that."

I remember how Greg agreed to coach me when no one else would, and I know Miyu's right. "There's more. Addison knows I was there and is threatening to tell Greg if I don't stay away from Braedon."

Miyu looks like she's eaten something sour. "That little . . ."

I can't help but giggle. That's the closest I've ever heard Miyu come to swearing. "I don't care about Braedon, but I hate the idea of Addison thinking I'm not talking to him because that's the way she wants it." I'm not entirely sure I don't care about Braedon, but maybe if I say it enough, I'll start to believe it.

"I'm with you there," Miyu says.

I take a deep breath and tell her what's been on my mind since I woke up this morning. "There's only one thing I can think of to do."

"What's that?" Miyu leans in a little closer.

"Tell Greg I did it. Just me. I'm not going to say anything about Braedon."

She's silent for a moment. "Wow. I don't know if that's crazy or brave. No, wait. It's crazy."

"I don't want to rat out Braedon, but I can't let Addison

use the whole thing to get what she wants. And I have to stop keeping these secrets. Even if it means that Mom will never let me out of the house again. Or agree to let me go to school."

"Do you want backup when you tell Greg?" Miyu asks.

I stop picking at my yoga mat. "You'd do that for me?"

"Of course!"

I shake my head. "I think this is something I have to do myself. But thank you."

"No matter what he says, at least you'll have it off your mind before Regionals," Miyu says.

Regionals. I can't believe the competition is next weekend. The whole thing with the Zamboni made me forget all about it. Until now. "Hey, I could use your help planning something for everyone before the competition."

"Sure. What are you thinking of? More bracelets?" Miyu scoots back around to my side as Karilee plugs in her boom box.

"Not a bracelet or anything like that. More like something to show everyone our club is just as good as any other club."

Her eyes get wide, and then a slow smile spreads across her face. "I'm in."

I find Miyu, Jessa, Samantha, Tom, Addison, and a whole bunch of other skaters in the Vocker Rooms before the four o'clock session on Monday. At least Braedon didn't show up. He's the last person I want to see right now.

"Hey, everyone! Kaitlin's here. She's going to tell you all about her plan," Miyu announces to the group.

Everyone's looking at me. I run my sweaty palms down the sides of my pants and take a deep breath as Braedon jogs in. Great.

"Go on, Kaitlin." Miyu elbows me in the side.

I force my mouth open and start talking. "Okay. So, you know how no one takes any of us seriously? All of the mean things they say when they think no one else is listening? The stuff that goes missing from our bags at competitions?"

A low grumble rolls through the group, and a few people nod.

"Miyu and I decided it's time we did something about that."

Miyu gives me a grin.

From his spot in the back of the group, Braedon raises his eyebrows, and the corners of his mouth turn up into a smile. I look past him and keep talking.

"I thought we could throw a party on Friday night at Regionals. Invite all the skaters. Show them that we like them and that we're fun to be around." I cross my fingers behind my back.

For a moment, no one says anything. Then Addison pipes up.

"A party?" She's standing off to the left in a red sweater and matching skating skirt. "Why would we want to throw a party for people who don't like us? Why don't we just have a party for ourselves?"

Some of the others nod in agreement.

"I know it's kind of a weird idea," I say. "But if we ever want things to change, I think we have to be the ones to make it happen."

"Sort of like taking the high road," Miyu adds.

"Exactly. If we're really nice and friendly to them, how can they keep being so mean to us?" My fingers are tingling, but I keep them crossed.

"I guess that makes sense," Tom says. "Sort of."

"It's not a sure thing, but our only other choice is just to let things go on as they are. And I don't know about you guys, but I'd rather try throwing a party."

No one says anything, but they're all looking at me like they're waiting to hear more.

"So if we do this, we have two big problems we need everyone's help with," I say.

"How to get people who hate us to come to our party?" Samantha asks.

"That's one. The other is where to have it. We'd have to pay to hold it in a restaurant. And no one's parents would want it in their hotel room." I don't add how much I wish Mom was the type who'd jump at the chance for her daughter to host a party. That would be so much easier than keeping this whole thing secret. And I have to, because no way would Mom go for this when it might distract me from preparing for competition.

"There's zero chance my mom will let me go to a party the night before I have to compete," a girl in a blindingly white dress says.

Others murmur in agreement. I try to block out images of Mom steaming mad after finding out I organized this whole thing. Across from Miyu, Addison's face is paler than pale. If there's any mom who'd be madder than mine, it would be hers.

"I can't tell my parents either," I say. "So maybe we should keep this a secret. Just invite the skaters. If they have fun, and they start being nicer to us, maybe their parents will too."

"But what if our parents find out?" the same girl asks.

I clear my throat, but my voice still trembles when I talk. "Look, guys, you know how mad my mom would be if she learned about the party, but I still want to do this. It's worth the risk to me to at least try to change everyone's minds. If we get other skaters thinking about how we're just like them, just as good as them—that we deserve it when we skate well and win—maybe they'll respect us. Maybe they'll stop calling us the Fall Down Club, and taking our things, and cutting us off in warm-up. We could actually have fun going to competitions if it wasn't for all those things."

I can't believe I said all that. The little girl in white is nodding and whispering to another girl next to her.

"Everyone who votes yes, raise your hand," Miyu says.

Every single hand shoots up. Did I just convince everyone to throw a party with me? Who am I, and what happened to the real Kaitlin?

"But how are we going to invite all the skaters?" Jessa asks. "If we go around and ask them, they'll laugh in our faces."

"Leave it to me." Braedon steps forward. "I know how to get an invite to every skater without them knowing who's throwing the party."

Miyu's glaring at him. I swallow the urge to say a bunch of rude stuff. If he can really do that, I need to let him. "Fine. Braedon will take care of the invitations," I say without looking at him.

"I still think it's a stupid idea," Addison says, leaning against the lockers.

"You voted yes," Miyu says.

Addison shrugs. "I like parties."

"Look, you don't have to be in on this." Miyu puts her hands on her hips. "We can all do it without you."

"Yeah, go sit at the snack bar while the rest of the club takes a stand," Jessa adds.

I'm totally with them. Who wants Addison's help? If she could even help at all, that is. She'd probably just stand around and complain that the party decorations are too cheap or the cupcakes aren't frosted fancy enough.

Addison narrows her eyes. "You're not leaving me out. Besides, I'm the only one who knows how you can have your loser party at the rink hosting Regionals. But if you don't want my help, then have fun standing around and eating Doritos in your hotel rooms alone."

I blink at her.

"What do you mean?" Miyu finally asks.

Addison shrugs. "I used to skate at the club there. I've been a member of almost every club in the region. And gotten uninvited from all of them too, thanks to my mom. Fallton was the only place left that would take me."

"How does that help anything?" I ask.

She smirks. "I was friends with one of the rink manager's daughters. She can probably get us one of their really nice party rooms."

The whole group is practically gaping at her. Who knew Addison could be the savior of Fallton?

If I ask nicely, that is.

"People would be way more likely to show up if they're already where the party is," Miyu says.

Addison nods and examines her nails, as if all the attention she's getting right now completely bores her.

"Would you call your friend and see if she can get us that room?" I ask as I cross my fingers behind my back again.

She picks at a tiny imperfection on her pink thumbnail. "I already said I would."

I uncross my fingers as Tom slaps Addison on the back and everyone smiles at her. Her eyebrows crinkle like she's not sure what to do or say now that everyone seems to like her.

She pulls out her phone. "I'll text her now."

While Addison waits for a reply from her friend in Indianapolis, the rest of us talk decorations and food. Tom and Samantha volunteer to buy it all, since ice dancers don't compete at Regionals and they'll miss out on the party. Just as we're debating between Fallton blue and white or more inclusive colors for the balloons, Greg opens the door to the Vocker Rooms.

"What's going on in here? Why aren't you all on the ice? The session started two minutes ago."

No one answers, but we all scramble to the door.

"Okay . . . ," Greg says as he watches us race toward the ice.

Addison stops next to me as I'm pulling off my blade guards. "Christina says she can get us the room. Turns out she has a job there now. And by the way, I'm glad you took my advice about Braedon."

I clench my hands into fists as she skates off. Just wait until she sees what I do after the sessions today. She won't feel so gloaty then.

Chapter Thirty

I don't even unlace my skates after the last session ends. Instead I wait by the doors for Greg to leave the ice after his lesson with Addison. Mom's busy chatting with Samantha's parents, so she doesn't even notice that I'm hanging around in my skates.

At least Dad isn't here to give me his disappointed eyes. It didn't happen for Praterville or me being late to Karilee's class. He seemed to think those things were kind of funny. But driving the Zamboni into the wall would probably be enough to bring out those what-happened-to-my-sweet-little-girl eyes. I don't think I could take that.

The Zam is fixed enough to putter across the ice again. I stand at the windows and watch it trace fat lines of smooth wet ice around and around. Something colorful catches my eye, and I press the side of my face against the cool window to look down the rows of bleachers.

It's Addison, in her red sweater and skating skirt. She's sitting on the bottom bleacher, way off to the right. She's talking to someone, and after a minute, an arm reaches around her shoulders to hug her. Swishy brown hair appears next to her fake blond ponytail.

Braedon. As if my stomach wasn't churning enough, seeing Braedon hugging Addison makes me feel even more sick.

I don't care about him. He's the one who got me into so much trouble, I say in my head. But I'm not sure I believe it.

I tear my eyes away from Braedon and Addison and try to steady my breathing. Is it even worth it to confess to Greg? Addison already seems to be getting her way.

It doesn't matter. If Braedon wants to hang out with Addison, fine. But I don't want it to be because she thinks she's blackmailing me. I really can't take all her smug, you-did-what-I-told-you looks.

And I don't think I can deal with this guilt anymore. Every time I see Greg, it threatens to eat me from the inside out. I barely made it through my lesson this morning without blurting it all out to him.

He finally steps into the lobby and stands for a moment, talking to Karilee. Miyu appears next to me and squeezes my hand. “I’m coming anyway,” she says. “I won’t say anything, but at least I’ll be there if you need me.”

I give her a grateful smile. It’s nice to have someone in my corner for a change. Greg and Karilee make their way through the rows of orange chairs. I put one skate in front of the other and catch Greg just as he’s saying hello to Mom.

I clear my throat. Miyu stands off to the side and gives me a thumbs-up.

“Mom, Greg, I have something I need to say.” My voice comes out all shaky. I take a deep breath and let the words go. “I was on the Zamboni last week when it crashed into the wall. I didn’t mean for anything to happen, but it did. It’s all my fault. I’m so sorry, and I won’t ever do anything like that again.”

Mom stares at me and grips her coffee cup so hard I’m afraid it will snap in two. Greg’s eyebrows knit together, and he shakes his head.

“Nice one, Kaitlin,” he says with a little laugh.

I twist my hands together. “I’m not kidding. I was on the Zam.”

"You were on the Zam?" Greg repeats.

"Kaitlin, you don't have to cover for whoever did this," Mom says quietly. "It was that Braedon, wasn't it?"

They aren't listening to me at all. I stomp my foot like a little kid. Annoyance boils up and flies out of my mouth as words. "I DID IT. I CRASHED THE ZAMBONI!"

Mom's looking at me like she's trying to figure out who I am. The chatter in the lobby dies down. I look to Miyu and notice Addison and Braedon standing just inside the doors, watching the whole thing. Greg turns and gives everyone a look, and the background noise starts again.

"Kaitlin, if you really did this . . . why?" Greg's staring me down.

I look away from his eyes and at the gritty floor. "I don't know. I guess I was curious. It was an accident."

"Hmm." Greg's quiet for a second. "Well, first, I'm very disappointed in you. I thought you knew better." The way he says it, I can tell he still doesn't believe me. "Second, you're going to have to do something to help pay the rink back for their costs."

"I don't mind." I can't look at Mom. I don't even want to know how much trouble I'm going to be in at home later. I can forget about ever going to school after this.

But Mom's surprisingly calm. She doesn't freak out at the rink. She doesn't yell at me in the car. It's not until we're almost home that she finally says something. And it's not even a lecture on how I'm throwing away my career and everything she and Dad worked so hard for.

"You've done a lot of things recently I never—*never*—in a million years thought my little girl would do. But crashing a Zamboni is not one of them." She gives me a sideways look from the driver's seat. "I'm pretty sure I know who you're covering for. And I don't want you hanging around him anymore."

I look out the window. "That won't be a problem." The fact that he didn't step in at all even though he heard me confessing the truth makes me want to never even look at him again.

Mom touches my arm lightly. "I'm worried about you, Kaitlin. You know you can talk to me."

"I'm fine." I wish I could cry on Mom's shoulder about everything—Braedon, having zero chance at Regionals, all the trouble I've gotten into. But she'd want to fix everything *her* way. Which would only make it all worse.

"I wish you'd tell Greg the truth."

"I did. I just want to concentrate on Regionals and forget this ever happened."

Mom sighs. "I can't argue with that."

Chapter Thirty-One

Before I know it, it's Friday and I'm following Mom through the Regionals chaos at the Indianapolis rink. I rub my eyes. I haven't been able to catch up on sleep, since I stayed up practically all night on Thursday plotting last-minute details for the party with Miyu and everyone else in the club. Between party planning, working on the most amazing gift I've ever thought of, avoiding Braedon, and skating practice, I've barely slept all week.

I try not to think about how my entire season—my entire career—hangs on this one competition. But weirdly enough,

I'm even more nervous about the party. Mostly about whether anyone will even show up.

My program. The practice session I'm about to step into. That's what I need to think about right now. Not the party, or how I'm going to completely lose Mom's trust in order to make it happen.

"What's going on, Kaitlin?" Greg asks as I glide to the boards to get a sip of water after crashing for the third time on my double axel. "You can do that jump in your sleep."

"Nerves, I guess." I shake my arms out. "Should I try it again?"

Greg shakes his head. "Wait until they play your music. Work on your footwork instead."

I skate away as he calls after me, "And emote!"

The rest of the practice doesn't go much better. Greg doesn't think I'm tango-y enough, the double axel is still a disaster, and I even manage to trip myself going into a camel spin.

"Get some rest today. I'll see you tomorrow," Greg says.

I sigh and pick up my stuff from the boards. If I skate like that during the qualifying round tomorrow, I'll totally deserve last place.

"You don't have anything to be nervous about," Dad says

when he and Mom meet me at the doors. "You're a great skater."

"Why don't we go back to the hotel, and you can walk through your program on the floor? That might help," Mom says.

I can't do that. We scheduled the party to start at five, and I have to meet everyone else from the club in ten minutes to decorate the party room. "I told Miyu I'd meet her for dinner at the snack bar. And then we're going to watch the competition together." The novice ladies' qualifying rounds are going on for the next few hours on the other ice surface. That should buy me just enough time. And Mom knows how much I love watching the higher levels.

"The snack bar?" Mom frowns. "That's not very healthy."

"They have fruit. And vegetable soup."

"That sounds fine to me," Dad says.

Mom gives him a look. "Okay. Dad and I will be back to pick you up at eight. You need a good night's rest for tomorrow."

"Thanks, Mom!" I race to the dressing room, leaving my parents staring after me. I yank my skates off, wipe them down as fast as I can, and throw my shoes on. I make sure to put everything in my locker this time.

Still in my practice dress, I squeeze through the crowd to a short hallway lined with rooms. Each door has a plastic sign on it with a goofy skating name: the Stick and Puck Room, the Triple Axel Room. The lights are on in the biggest room at the very end—the Olympic Room. I peek into the windowed door, and . . . wow.

Inside, Miyu, Jessa, Addison, and a bunch of other kids from the club are running around, moving tables and chairs and hanging up decorations. No Braedon. I push open the door and step in.

"What do you think?" Miyu's arranging some two-liter soda bottles on a table.

I hug my arms against my damp dress. "It's amazing. Addison really hooked us up. This isn't at all what I expected." I take in the giant TV, the stereo system, and the disco ball hanging from the ceiling.

"I know, right? Wait till you see the different-colored lights."

"I'm sorry I'm late." Seeing everyone working so hard to pull off this party more than makes up for the awful practice I just had.

Miyu waves a hand at me. "You're not. I just thought we could get started while you had your practice."

"Kaitlin, finally!" Addison walks up to me in a huff, with an older girl I don't recognize. "You're still in your practice clothes? Gross. Who wears a sweaty skating dress to a party?"

I ignore her. Nothing she can say bothers me now. Besides, we're at a skating rink party, not a tea party at the Plaza Hotel. Although Addison could totally show up there in her pink skirt and sweater. And is that a real diamond pendant necklace?

"Hello? Christina needs that movie or whatever it is you want put on the TV." Addison points to the seriously huge wide-screen on the wall, with a little skate icon dancing around as a screen saver.

"I have it." Miyu pulls the DVD from her pocket and hands it to Addison. "Thanks . . . Christina?"

"Yeah, I work here," Christina says. She tucks a strand of long black hair behind an ear. "Used to skate with Addy until she left us for you guys."

"Addy?" I say once Christina's left with the DVD.

Addison narrows her eyes. "Call me that and die."

"Has anyone seen Braedon?" Not that I want to see him, but I really hope he was able to get invitations out to everyone. Otherwise, this is all pointless.

Miyu shakes her head.

A hint of a smile flits across Addison's face. That gloaty, smug smile. "I just talked to him. He's taking care of the invitations."

"Great. Hey, I think Jessa needs help with the streamers." Miyu points across the room.

Addison takes the hint, giving me one last smirk before she leaves.

"Can't we uninvite her?" I ask Miyu. I know I don't care anymore if Addison likes Braedon or he likes her, and I have the upper hand since I owned up to the Zamboni crash. But still. That doesn't mean I want to actually spend time in the same room as her.

"Probably not. I mean, since she got us this room and she's part of Fallton and everything. Unfortunately." Miyu hands me a bag of chips and a bowl.

I pour the chips into the bowl—and a few into my mouth, since I'm starving. Everyone's talking, and I can practically feel their excitement about the party. I close my eyes and will that excitement to push away all my worries—my program, Mom finding out about this party, the fear that no one will even show up to the party, the thought that I still might kind of like Braedon even though he's a total jerk.

"Kaitlin, I know that practice was exhausting, but you seriously cannot take a nap right now." Miyu thrusts a box of cookies into my hands.

I finish helping Miyu with the food. At five o'clock,

everything is ready. The Olympic Room has silver stars and streamers and balloons in every color hanging from the ceiling. Samantha sent along some amazing signs for the walls that say things like, SKATE GREAT! and JUMP HIGH! SPIN FAST! Music pumps from the speakers. And on the huge TV, the video I made runs on a loop.

"You guys, this is . . . it's incredible." I turn around so no one can see me wipe away the tears that popped up.

"It was your idea," Jessa says. "We only helped."

"And I told you it was a bad idea," Addison says from next to the TV. "See, it's past five, and no one's here. They aren't coming."

I cross fingers on both of my hands in the hopes that Braedon actually invited everyone. Anyone competing in novice ladies obviously won't be here, since that's happening now, but there are still four other levels of skaters, plus everyone from the lower levels doing the nonqualifying competition—hundreds of kids. Where are they? Minutes tick by, and still no one shows up. I feel a little sick to my stomach. If everyone went through this much trouble for the party, and we don't have any guests . . . I'll feel awful.

"What are we going to do if no one comes?" I ask Miyu.

"Well, I think we should still have the party. All of Fallton is here, and we already have food and music. Who cares if no one else comes? We'll show them what they're missing." She's actually grinning at me.

I smile back. She's right. Why let a good party go to waste? It won't be the same, but we can still have fun. But now I wish I'd taken an extra five minutes and put something else on. I'm freezing in my damp practice dress.

"Someone's coming!" a younger girl shouts from the door.

"Quick, everyone act like we're having the best time in the world," I say. People group off and start talking and laughing like we've been party-hardy this whole time.

Braedon appears in the doorway. "What'd I miss?"

One of the older guys groans. "It's just Braedon," he announces. "Dude, we thought you were one of the other skaters."

"They're coming," Braedon says. "Don't worry about that. They all got a text message about an hour ago."

"How did you get everyone's phone numbers?" Miyu asks.

I'm pretty sure it involved stealing or hacking into someone's computer. Otherwise, Braedon wouldn't have volunteered for the job.

"I might've borrowed the contact list for the entire competition," he says.

Borrowed. Right.

“You realize the phone numbers on that list are probably for parents?” Miyu says.

Braedon shrugs. “Doesn’t matter. I already heard buzz building in the lobby about the party. They’ll be here.”

If their parents don’t blab on us to our parents. Leave it to Braedon to get everyone into trouble. I busy myself with rearranging the plates and cups on the closest table and wish he would just go away.

No luck. He’s breathing over my shoulder. “This is a great idea, Double Axel.”

“Don’t call me that,” I say through clenched teeth.

“Sorry. Anything else I can do to help?” He’s acting like everything is completely normal.

“No.”

He’s silent for a moment, and I kind of hope that means he’ll take the hint and disappear.

“Wow, that’s an awful clip of my triple salchow,” he says.

I turn around. He’s watching my video on the TV, and he’s got his joking face on. But this is Braedon—always saying or doing something that hurts someone else. “I made that video,” I tell him.

He drops the smile. “I’m sorry. I didn’t realize it was you. It’s a good video, really.”

I ignore him and rub my hands on my arms to try to warm up.

"Are you cold? Do you need a jacket?" he asks.

"No, I don't need your jacket." I drop my arms and take a step toward the door to see if anyone might be coming.

He taps me on the shoulder. "Kaitlin, what's wrong? I've barely seen you all week."

"Nothing," I say without turning around.

He steps in front of me. "Are you mad about the Zam?"

I look around him.

"You know, you're really annoying sometimes," he says. "If you're angry at me, just say it already."

Irritation rises up inside me and threatens to spill, the way it did in Praterville and when Mom and Greg wouldn't listen to me about the Zamboni. "Why are you here? You don't care about the competition or the club or me or even your own skating."

Braedon takes a step back. "I care about the club. Didn't I just invite everyone to this party? And . . . I thought we were friends."

The words fly out of my mouth before I even realize what I'm saying. "Really? Then why are you always doing stupid things and getting me in trouble? I should've known when I followed you doing that chicken dance and almost broke

Addison's nose. But I thought you liked— Never mind." My face goes warm.

He crosses his arms. "We were just having fun."

"And crashing the Zamboni was fun?" All the chill from wearing a wet dress is gone, and my skin feels like it's sizzling.

"Well, not that part. But no one even knew we were there. At least they didn't until you told Greg."

I laugh. A few of the people around us stop talking.

But I don't really care. I'm on fire and I need to throw some sparks at Braedon. "That's funny. Ha-ha. Who knows what kind of job I'm going to have to do to pay back the rink? But don't worry, no one knows *you* were there. Except Addison, and she doesn't care."

Braedon turns to look at Addison, who's suddenly really interested in the tape holding one of Samantha's signs to the wall.

"Why did you tell on yourself?" he asks me in a soft voice.

"I had to. I'm not like you. It turns out that I can't go around lying and pretending everything is okay when it's not. Now, if you don't mind, I need to see if anyone is coming." I take a step toward Miyu, who's moved in close like she's ready to jump in and yell at Braedon if I need her to. "And please leave me alone," I toss over my shoulder.

Miyu walks with me toward the door. We step out into the empty hallway. "Are you all right?" she asks.

I let out a breath. "I think so. I can't believe I said all that." The heat is gone, and I'm freezing again. I'm light-headed and my legs are like jelly. But I feel good, as if I can do anything in the world.

"You should do that more often," Miyu says.

Maybe she's right.

"No one's coming. Let's just go in and enjoy the party." She takes my hand, and just as we're about to slide back into the room, I spot someone.

A few someones, actually. And they're headed straight toward our party.

Chapter Thirty-Two

Miyu and I race back inside, and a few seconds later, a group of girls that I recognize from a club in Ohio are standing just inside the doorway.

"There's no one here. Just those Fall Down kids," one of them says.

"Hey, look, they've got brownies!" Another girl leaps away from the group and scoops up one of the brownies that Jessa brought from home.

The first girl shrugs, and the entire group moves farther into the room.

"Let's go talk to them," Miyu says.

But Addison's already beat us over there. She's offering them drinks and complimenting their clothes. In less than a minute, she's laughing with the girl who wanted to turn around and leave.

"Who knew Addison could be so friendly?" I say to Miyu.

The room fills up as more and more skaters arrive. By six o'clock, there are so many people crammed into the Olympic Room that I've finally stopped shivering. Everywhere I turn, people are talking or laughing or dancing. Braedon's doing some crazy break-dancing thing in the corner while a couple of other guys egg him on. Of course he has to be the center of attention.

And I've met skaters from as far away as Alabama. One of them even told me how much she loved my new music when she heard it at practice earlier.

"Thanks, but I have trouble really getting into it," I told her.

"My program music is this super-sad piece," she said. "And the only way I can pull it off is to remember how I felt when my dog died last year. It's like I'm torturing myself for skating, but it works, you know?"

Actually, I don't know, because I've never thought about skating like that.

One of the guys break-dancing with Braedon crashes into

a table and knocks a bowl of chips onto the floor. I start toward the spilled chips when I spot someone I recognize watching the enormous TV.

I cross my fingers and move toward her. "Hey, Peyton?"

"What's this video?" she asks.

"It's . . . um . . . well, I went online and found a bunch of clips from a lot of the skaters here. And I made them into this video." I don't add that it took me hours to find and cut all those clips, and to select the music and decide how to group them all under captions like *Grace* and *Athleticism* and *Ambition*.

"Hey, that's me!" She smiles at the clip of herself landing a perfect double flip. Then she turns to me. "So you did this? You were always making things for everyone. I still use that water bottle, you know."

A warm, happy feeling fills me up from head to toe. "I made a copy of the video for everyone to pick up when they leave." I point to the stack of DVDs on a table near the door.

"Thanks," Peyton says. "Did you plan this party? I thought it was something official."

"No, it was me. Me and everyone else at Fallton. We just wanted to throw a party for all the competitors."

Peyton's red hair falls into her face. She searches for an

elastic in her pocket and pulls her hair into a ponytail. "That's really . . . nice of you guys. I mean, considering, you know?"

I know exactly what she means, which is the point of this whole thing. "We just wanted everyone to have a chance to have fun and maybe meet other skaters."

"So how are things at the Fall D—sorry—Fallton?"

"Really good. Everyone's friendly, and my new coach is the best." And I realize it's true. I love skating at Fallton, despite everything else. In fact, if Ridgeline asked me back, I'd probably say no. I have friends at Fallton, which is something I never really had at my old club. "So . . . is Ellery here?"

"Her mom wouldn't let her come. Which is too bad, because this is a blast. Hey, who's that cute guy with the crazy dance moves?" Peyton points toward one of Braedon's new friends, someone I met earlier from another Michigan club.

"Go talk to him. I think his name is Ian." I give her little push, and she turns back and grins at me.

"Hey, Kaitlin?" Miyu's standing behind me, holding the stack of DVDs. "I think we should hand these out now. Otherwise people might forget to pick them up when they leave."

Miyu and I weave through groups of people, passing out DVDs left and right. Every time someone says, "Great party!" my heart feels like it's going to burst.

"This is actually working," I say to Miyu as we squeeze between people near the drinks.

"I can't believe how crowded it is. And everyone's having fun, and they're talking to us like actual people instead of telling us to literally break a leg," Miyu replies.

We're so busy handing out DVDs that we don't even notice the big man with the Indianapolis Ice polo shirt until we almost run into him.

"Um, hi," I say. "Are you here for the party?" Even if their parents got Braedon's text, no one had brought their mom or dad.

"P-party?" the man sputters. "You can't be here!"

Miyu crinkles her eyebrows at him. "But we have the room reserved."

"For a competitors' party," I add.

"No one reserved this room." He cups his hands around his mouth. "Party's over! Move it out. Now!"

A few people look at him, and then go right back to talking.

"Can't we stay a little longer? We won't be here very late," I ask. He can't end the party now, not while everyone's having fun. Because then what would people think of us?

"Not if you didn't reserve the room and pay for it."

"Pay?" I repeat. But he's already marching through the crowd.

"Wait!" Miyu shouts. We look at each other and race behind him toward the stereo.

He hits a button and the music dies. "Thank you for coming. Now get out or your parents will get a bill for the use of this room."

His words echo across the room. Everyone's still for a second, and then they all make for the door.

"Not you two." The man points to me and Miyu. "You stay put." He studies Miyu's Fallton jacket and starts texting on his phone. This is not good.

"What's going on?" Jessa's fought through everyone streaming toward the door to reach me and Miyu.

"He says we can't have the room. It wasn't reserved or something." I sneak a glance up at him as he watches everyone leaving. "You guys should get out while you can. I think we're in huge trouble."

Jessa crosses her arms. "I'm not going anywhere."

"Me either." Braedon's joined her, along with just about everyone else in Fallton.

"It was going so well," one of the younger girls says. "And now they'll all hate us again because the party got cut short."

"I think that's the least of our worries," Braedon adds. He nods at the big man. "Hey, mister, what's the big deal here?"

"The big deal, *kid*, is that you and your friends are throwing an unauthorized party in a room you shouldn't be in, and that no one has paid for, and serving food and drinks that were not purchased from our snack bar." The man looks over our heads at my video, playing on the TV. "And you're using extremely expensive electronic equipment without permission."

"We did too reserve the room. And the TV." Addison pushes her way to the front. With her hands on her hips, she looks like her mom.

"You did not, young lady. I'm the assistant manager. I keep the calendar of reservations."

"Just ask Christina. She works here."

"Christina?" The man looks confused for a moment. "You mean the general manager's daughter? She's not an employee."

Addison's confident face drops a little. "She told me she was. And that she reserved this room for us."

"Did you pay her?"

"Um . . . no." Addison bites her lip.

"Then you didn't reserve the room. And Christina has no authority to do so anyway."

Addison's face goes red. I feel awful for her, so I reach over and touch her arm. "Hey, it's okay."

She jerks her arm away. "I didn't do anything wrong. I only talked to Christina because *you* asked me to."

"Addison, we're all in this together," Jessa says quietly. "It's no one's fault."

I turn to the man. "I'm sorry we didn't get the room the right way. We'll clean everything up, and it'll look like we've never been here." *And please, please, please don't tell our parents about this,* I want to add. I cross my fingers and hope he'll go for it.

"You bet you'll clean this up. And there's who I've been waiting for." I follow his gaze to the door, where a woman in the same Indianapolis Ice polo has walked in with Greg and Karilee.

I want to disappear into the floor and become one with the carpet. As if I'm not in enough trouble with Greg after the Zamboni crash, now he'll think I'm some crazy party girl who isn't serious at all about skating. Kind of like Braedon. And he'll definitely tell all of our parents.

Greg looks from the group of us to the TV and then back to the rink employee. "What is this all about?"

"Your kids threw an illicit party," the big man says.

"Illicit" makes it sound a lot more awful than just a bunch of skaters hanging out and talking. My stomach is doing axels while I wait for Greg to say something. If only we could explain to him why we had the party. Somewhere deep down, I think he'd understand. Maybe even be supportive. After all, it's his club too. His skaters, his name on the line every time one of us takes the ice in front of a rink full of people who think we aren't good enough.

But if he doesn't feel that way, then what? I don't think he'll kick me out of the club. If he didn't for the Zamboni, then he won't for doing this.

At least I hope not.

Greg rubs his eyes with his right hand, as if we're all a vision that will go away. I take a deep breath. At the worst, Mom will ground me for eternity when she finds out, and Greg will lecture me about competition decorum. And I can forget about going to school.

But it *has* to be worth it. If we didn't try, we'd never know what could've happened. People were having fun before the party got busted.

Karilee smiles and twists her hands together. "I don't think they meant any harm. It's just a party. A chance for those with similar interests to support and give strength to one another."

The big man crosses his arms. "We aren't against parties. Only those that were thrown without following the appropriate procedures."

"Which are?" Greg asks.

"Reserving the room with management, and paying for it." The man glares at us.

"Fine. How much is it?" Greg pulls a wallet from his pant pocket.

"Five hundred dollars."

Greg blinks at him. "Come again?"

"Five hundred dollars," the man says again. "This is our biggest room, with state-of-the-art equipment and brand-new lighting fixtures. The fee also includes the food and drinks that should've been purchased here."

Greg folds up his wallet. "Look, I'm sorry they used the room and didn't reserve it. On a competition night. Without asking their coaches or their parents." He's scowling at us as he says this.

I scoot closer to Miyu.

"I assure you they will clean all of this up and then some. And I'll be certain to let their parents know of this situation. But nothing's broken or missing, and the party's over. Can we leave it at that?"

"We can as soon as someone pays me for the use of this room. Or I'll have no choice but to ban you all from this rink."

Everyone starts talking all at once. Some protest, a couple of girls start crying, and Braedon yells, "That's not fair!"

My whole body is shaking. I *have* to compete. It's my only chance at going to Nationals. Not to mention everyone else's. Miyu's tried so hard to get her double lutz consistent, and this is Jessa's year to make a comeback. Addison's face is paper white. Her mother will probably disown her if she can't compete.

"If you get me kicked out of Regionals, Kaitlin, I'll never forgive you," Addison whispers.

"It's not her fault. You went along with it." Miyu glares at Addison.

Greg holds his hands up, like he's surrendering or something, and speaks over the top of everyone else. "I understand why you're angry. But isn't a ban a little . . . excessive? Some of these kids are competing tomorrow, for their one and only shot at Nationals this year."

"I don't care if they're all shoo-ins for gold at the Olympics," the man says. "Someone needs to pay this rink five hundred dollars."

I don't have five hundred dollars, and I'm sure no one else does either.

"This didn't work at all," I whisper to Miyu. "It's a complete disaster. Everyone's getting kicked out of the competition, and it's my fault!"

Miyu swipes at her eyes. "I'm just as responsible. I helped come up with the idea."

I shake my head. "If it wasn't for me, this wouldn't have happened at all. I have to say something so they don't kick everyone out."

"Kaitlin," Miyu says, but I don't let her finish.

I step forward and clench my hands to stop them from trembling. Svetlana's voice echoes in my head. *You think you are shy girl. But you are not.*

I can do this. I was the one who told the judges exactly how I felt at Praterville. I told off Braedon, too. Besides, even if I have to confess, I can tell Greg why we threw the party, and maybe at least he won't toss me out of the club. I don't know where I'll get the money for the room, but I'll figure something out. The most important thing right now is to let everyone compete.

I look the assistant manager straight in his eyes. I clear my throat and say, as loud as I can, "I have to tell you something."

The room quiets. Greg tilts his head, as if I'm the last person he'd expect to speak up right now. "What is it, Kaitlin?"

"I . . ." My voice shakes. I take a breath and start again. "The party was my—"

"I did it. The whole thing was my idea," Braedon blurts out as he pushes past me.

Chapter Thirty-Three

"I thought it would be good for everyone to let off some steam, and we wanted to show the other skaters that we're just like them," Braedon says. "I'm the one who got Addison to ask Christina for the room. I'm the one who used the TV and the stereo and brought in the outside food. I'll pay for the room. Just don't kick anyone else out."

Everyone stares at Braedon. I can't let him pay for something I did. I want to speak up, but Miyu tugs on my arm. *Let him*, she mouths.

I step back and wait in stunned silence as Greg finally says something. "Braedon, where are you going to get that kind of money?"

"I'll withdraw from the competition. Get a refund."

Withdraw? He can't do that. "Braedon—" I start to say.

"And then I'll ask my mom to use the rest of the money she had set aside for my coaching fees and competition videos."

"If that's not enough, I'll cover the rest," Greg says to the assistant manager. "And you can pay me back, Braedon."

"I suppose that'll work. Just make sure this room is spotless." The assistant manager hands a card to Greg before he leaves with the other employee.

Greg shoves the card into a pocket. He scans the lot of us, his eyes landing on Braedon. "I don't know what you were thinking, doing this on a competition night without asking me or your parents. But at least you stepped up and did the right thing."

Karilee snaps her fingers. "All right, everyone. Let's get this place back into shape." They all slowly move toward the tables. But I hang back.

Braedon shifts his weight. He actually looks uncomfortable, which I didn't even think was possible. "I'm sorry I wasted your time preparing for Regionals, and now I can't compete," he says quietly to Greg.

"This behavior needs to stop, Braedon. Immediately. There's only so much I and everyone else can put up with. You nearly cost the entire club this competition." Greg looks dead serious. I swallow hard, knowing Braedon's only hearing this because of me.

Braedon nods but doesn't say anything.

Greg and Karilee leave, probably to tell all of our parents about the party. As soon as they're gone, everyone starts talking again.

I march straight to Braedon. "Why did you do that?"

"I don't mind not competing," he says with a shrug. "I thought you would be really upset if you couldn't skate here, so I took the blame. I was just as much a part of it as you and everyone else, anyway."

Tears sting my eyes. I squeeze my eyelids shut to make them go away. "You didn't have to do that."

"Don't get so worked up," he says, grinning. "It's okay. Besides, I have a reputation to uphold. I couldn't let you upstage me."

I let out a short laugh. "I guess we're even, then."

"By the way, I'm going to tell Greg about the Zamboni, too. Maybe we can work the skate rental together to make up for it?" His hair falls into his eyes, and he pushes it out of the way.

I wrinkle my nose. "The skate rental? Yuck."

"Or maybe we'll have to clean toilets."

"Ugh, that's not funny!"

"Friends again?" He holds out a trash bag from a box Miyu must've remembered to bring.

"Friends. But if you want to do anything stupid, you're on your own." As I start filling the bag with dirty cups and napkins, I remember how he was hugging Addison on the bleachers back home. At least we can be friends, even if he likes her in a more-than-friends way.

"Hey, Kaitlin," Braedon says. "Skate great tomorrow, okay?"

"I still can't believe he did that. I never expected Braedon to be so . . ." Miyu trails off, searching for the right word.

"Gallant?" I supply. That's the word my dad used to describe Jack at the end of *Titanic*, when he put Rose on a piece of furniture floating in the ocean while he stayed in the cold water to freeze. Even though Regionals is hardly life and death, I kind of feel like Rose right now.

"That's it. He's just always been so selfish."

"Yeah." I retie the laces on my left skate for the third time. First they were too loose, then too tight. "I just wish the party had worked. Having it end early probably made everyone mad at us."

"Girls! Your warm-up is next." Mom bursts through the doors as I stand up to shake out my left foot. I got a good, long lecture from her about wasting my potential by going to parties when I should be resting for competition. But no grounding this time, because she has no idea I masterminded the whole thing.

At least I get to compete, thanks to Braedon. It's weird how he was the one getting me into trouble, and now it's my idea that made him withdraw from the competition.

Miyu and I duck through the doors and hop onto the ice when our warm-up is called. We both made it through the qualifying round yesterday, scoring well enough to get into the championship round, along with Addison and Ellery.

"I'm glad we're in the same group," Miyu says as we hand our guards to Karilee and Greg. "Moral support and all."

I grin at her and then take off around the rink, trying not to think about how much is riding on my performance today. The ice is a little rough from the first group of girls in our division. But it's good ice—smooth and not too bumpy.

I move through my spins and jumps. Everything was a hundred times better in qualifying yesterday and in my morning practice than it was before the party on Friday. In the qualifying round, I got just over 23 points for my technical score. But just 9.06 for my program components, which is only a teeny-tiny bit better than Chicago. Whatever it is the judges are looking for, I still don't have it.

As I glide off the ice, I can tell Greg isn't happy.

"Kaitlin, listen," Greg says as I wait for the announcer to call my name. "You have to stop thinking about what you think you can't do. Dig in deep and find that girl who isn't afraid to show everyone who she is."

"I don't know . . . ," I say to Greg. I feel all jittery, and for the millionth time, I wish I'd stuck with *Swan Lake*.

"You wouldn't have picked this music if it wasn't right for you," he says. "You *can* do this. Show them how badly you want to go to Nationals."

The announcer calls my name and I glide toward center ice, raising my arms. Braedon and everyone from the club cheer for me from somewhere high up in the bleachers.

But there's more. More cheering than usual. Someone yells, "Go, Kaitlin!" and it's not from the Fallton clump at the top of the stands.

Why would people cheer for me after our party got busted?

I stop, and the scraping sound from my blades echoes through the rink. I do a little turn, not wanting the music to start yet.

This is it. This is my only chance to qualify for Nationals this year. I know I don't stand a chance, not if the judges think I can't interpret my music. But if I skate the best I can, at least I'll know I couldn't have done any better. Maybe Mom will let me go to school. Dad will be proud. Greg will be happy he's my coach, even though I've made some stupid decisions lately.

And I have to do it for Braedon, at the very least.

The music starts, and I look straight out at the audience. A few last-minute cheers die out. I give my best flirty smile and launch into the first steps of the program.

"Yeah, Kaitlin!" Braedon shouts from the bleachers.

People in the front row echo him. I don't even know who they are.

The music pounds out a rhythm that reaches into my soul. I never realized how fun this music is. The beat moves into my body and stretches my arms out as I reach toward the judges before I start the footwork.

I don't even have to think about each individual jump and spin. Instead they flow out of the music as I leap and turn across the ice. I feel like I did on Friday night, as I wove through the crowd at the party, talking to people I never would've even said hello to before. I stretch into the spread eagle that I chose for this very moment in the program. People are cheering as I hold the long edge with both my feet turned out, but I can barely hear them over the pounding of the music in my head.

The rhythm of the music stays the same, but the tone changes. Instead of flirty, now it's angry. I charge down the ice as I remember exactly how I felt when I got my scores at Praterville. How I felt when I saw Braedon sitting with Addison. I attack the double axel like it's the last time I'll ever do one.

And land it perfectly.

I want to laugh and yell and cry at the same time, but the music is telling me what to do. I've let it carry me through the entire program. Before I even realize it, the last notes echo through the rink. I stop and toss my head as if I can't possibly spare the time for anyone in the audience. Then I give them a sly smile.

Applause erupts all around me. Everyone is clapping and

shouting—not just my friends and family. I spin around and curtsy to the judges, then the audience. And only then do I let the smile take over my face.

"You got it!" Greg says the second I jump off the ice.

"I didn't think about the elements. I remembered how much fun I had at the party, and how I felt when I got my scores at Praterville. And then it just happened!"

"All you had to do was let go and let the feelings take over. And it worked. You had the audience the entire time."

"Wow, Kaitlin! That was amazing!" Miyu grabs me into a hug.

I go from her hug into Mom's. "Perfect. It doesn't matter where the judges put that, I'm so proud of you."

"You looked like you were having so much fun," Dad says from over Mom's shoulder.

"I was." I don't remember competing being fun before. I did it more for the results, not because I liked it.

I hate to admit it, but maybe the judges were right. Maybe there was something missing from my performances before this. I just never understood it because I'd never felt it before.

Now if only the judges saw what I felt as I skated.

Mom's holding one of my hands, and Miyu has the other

as we wait for my scores to be announced. I cross my toes inside my skates. I've never wanted anything more in my life than to qualify for Nationals.

"Come on, come on," Dad says from behind me. I turn around, and he's tapping his fingers on either side of his coffee cup. Dad never gets this worked up about my skating.

The announcer's voice booms over the speakers. "The scores for Kaitlin Azarian-Carter are . . ."

Chapter Thirty-Four

Mom grips my hand harder.

"The technical elements score is 24.75. The program components score is 18.02. The total segment score for Kaitlin is 42.77. She is currently in first place through seven skaters."

I can't move. Did I hear it right—42.77? First place? Me?!

Greg propels us all into the lobby. Miyu drops my hand and flies into me so hard I almost fall over.

"Kaitlin! You did it!" She's squeezing me in a hug and jumping up and down at the same time. She's squealing, and it finally hits me.

I got a good score. Not just a good score . . . a great score!

A Nationals-qualifying-type score. I scream and grab Miyu back and jump up and down with her.

"You're going to Nationals!" she shouts.

Mom's wiping tears from her eyes, and Dad's grinning and patting me on the shoulder.

"We don't know that for sure," Greg says, but he's smiling like crazy. "There are still five more girls left to skate. Including you, Miyu, so you'd better go find Karilee."

Miyu gives me one last hug and runs back into the rink.

Greg puts a hand on each of my shoulders. "No matter how everyone else does, I'm proud of you. You put every ounce of yourself into that program, and it showed."

"Thanks," I say. I can't stop smiling. I've done everything I could. Now I just have to wait and see what everyone else does.

"Hey, nice score!" a girl I recognize from the party last night says as she walks by. "Maybe I'll see you in Denver, at Nationals."

"That was awfully nice," Mom says.

"Huh . . . it was. . . ." Greg watches as the girl disappears into the crowd.

I guess she didn't mind that the party ended early.

Mom and Dad go back in with me to watch Miyu's program. I'd never noticed how graceful she is. She sweeps up and down the ice like a ballerina. Her program isn't perfect; she misses a couple of jumps. But no one can beat her in sheer beauty. When she finishes, I scream and clap as loud as I can. And so does everyone else, not just the kids from Fallton. When her scores are announced, they won't get her to Nationals, but she's happy.

"It's okay," she says, completely out of breath from her skate. "I messed up those jumps something awful."

"Excuse me, I have to get to the ice." Ellery bumps by us without a second glance.

I watch her step out and hand her blade guards to Hildy. I can't believe I ever thought of her as a friend. I didn't know what a real friend was, I guess.

"Who cares about the jumps?" I say to Miyu. "You looked beautiful out there. It was like ballet on ice."

Miyu smiles at me, and we grab seats near our parents to finish watching the competition.

Ellery skates a near-perfect program and knocks me down a place.

"But just barely," Miyu says.

"She outscored you on program components," Mom adds. "No one can touch your technical score."

"No one else has a double axel," I finish for her in my best imitation-Mom voice.

"You bet," Mom says.

Addison is the last to skate, and by that time, my score has been bumped down to fourth place. But fourth place is okay. It's more than okay, actually. Fourth place means I still get to go to Nationals.

Fifth place, however, doesn't.

I clap and cheer for Addison along with everyone else.

"Everyone's really enthusiastic today," Mom says. "I don't think this many people cheered for you guys in Chicago."

"I'm pretty sure they didn't," I say. Mom looks at me like she's waiting for me to explain, but I don't feel like talking about the party again. I'll only end up with another lecture.

Addison's music starts, and I sit on crossed fingers. I don't know what I'm hoping for. As much as I don't like Addison, I don't want her to fail. But I really want to go to Nationals. Her *Phantom of the Opera* program is dramatic and strong, and she lands all her jumps. She finishes with a smile.

It seems like forever until Addison's scores are announced. When the announcer finally comes on, I don't hear anything until, "42.01."

"Wait, is that lower or higher than me?" I ask.

"Addison is in fifth place," the announcer answers for me. "This ends the juvenile girls' division. The next event will begin in thirty minutes."

"You finished fourth," Dad says.

"Fourth!" I echo.

I did it. I snagged the last spot to Nationals! I beat out Addison by one place.

"Kaitlin!" Mom screams. She jumps up from her spot on the bleachers and snatches me in a bear hug, practically crushing my lungs.

Dad is grinning from ear to ear, and Greg comes running across the mats.

"You qualified," Greg says. "You're going to Denver!" He slaps me on the back and almost knocks me over before leaving to find his students in the next event.

On our way out of the rink, we pass Addison and . . . is that her mom? I don't think I've ever seen her smiling. Like really, truly, actually smiling. She's even hugging Addison, who looks like she's going to cry from happiness.

"I guess fifth place is good enough for Addison's mom," I say to Miyu.

"She's probably secretly hoping one of the top girls comes

down with a nasty flu, so Addison can take her place at Nationals," Miyu replies.

"Hey, Kaitlin!" Braedon's voice calls over the crowd in the lobby. I spot him next to a table full of new colorful blade guards. "That was amazing! You're going to Nationals." He pushes his hair out of his eyes and gives me a warm smile.

"Thanks," I say. "I wouldn't have been able to skate without what you did." I glance at Mom to see if she's about to stomp over and make Braedon leave. But Miyu's steered her toward a table of skating keepsakes.

Braedon waves his hand like it's no big deal. "That party was a great idea. And it worked."

It was so nice to hear cheers when I skated. "I don't understand why, though. I mean, we had to end it early. I thought people would be really mad about that."

"Are you kidding?" Braedon says. "They went to a party that got busted by rink management. It was exciting!"

"Huh." I never thought of it that way.

Braedon drops his smile. "You know, I owed you for getting you into so much trouble."

"Thanks, but it wasn't all your fault. I went along with it all—the Zam, skipping dance class, everything." I pull my jacket tighter around myself. I don't care who sees the club name now. I'm proud to be a member of Fallton.

"But you wouldn't have done any of those things if I hadn't talked you into them. Sometimes I don't think about stuff like that. I don't see past the fun of it all."

"That's your story, isn't it?"

He blinks at me. "My what?"

"Remember when I first started at Fallton? You told me everyone there has a story." I point at him.

Braedon pushes his hair back. "Oh, right. The other clubs I skated with didn't think my pranks were so funny. And for some reason, they really wanted me to show up to every single session. Not do fun stuff like run off to get Cokes right before off-ice."

"It was fun," I admit. "But maybe we shouldn't crash things or climb out of windows at sleepovers."

He raises his eyebrows. "Speak for yourself, Double Axel," he says.

I realize he's flirting with me again, which doesn't make any sense. "Did you see Addison got fifth?" I nod toward where she and Mrs. Thomas have come in from the rink.

"That should make her mother happy," he says.

"I thought my mom could get a little too worked up about skating, but she doesn't have anything on Addison's," I say as

I watch Mrs. Thomas open that notebook she always has and start pointing out things Addison could do even better the next time. Addison's smile disappears.

"A few days before we left, her mom made her cry," Braedon says. "Can you believe that? Something about how if Addison didn't do well here, her mom was pulling her out of skating. She's really been on her case about landing the double axel, too. I was trying to help her with it."

"Oh." Pieces of a puzzle are clicking together in my head. "Wait, was she crying out on the bleachers earlier this week?"

"Yeah," Braedon says. "Why?"

"Nothing. I just . . . I think I saw her out there is all." I feel a little light-headed as I remember Braedon hugging Addison that afternoon. It wasn't because he likes her. He was trying to make her feel better about her mom. "Wait, is that how you got her not to tell on me for skipping dance class? Promised to help her with her double axel?"

He nods. "Hey, maybe when we get back, we can hang out again?" he says. "I promise I won't make you late to anything."

I smile at him. "You forget we'll be hanging out a lot, scrubbing toilets."

"I meant something a little more fun than that."

"Yeah, that would be great." And it would be. Just as long

as I don't confuse having fun with making dumb decisions.

Braedon reaches out a hand. "Jessa's group is up next. Let's go see if we can be the loudest people in the bleachers when she takes the ice."

I take his hand and smile. And, in a weird way, I'm glad I messed up so badly at Praterville. If I hadn't, I would've never met Braedon, Miyu, or any of the others.

Not knowing them would be a lot worse than not qualifying for Nationals.

Chapter Thirty-Five

The results get even better as the day goes on. Jessa wins the senior division and qualifies for Sectionals, which is one more step before Nationals for higher levels. Everyone from our club seems to be riding the momentum of the party. I'm so happy about how things turned out, but something is still hanging over me.

I think about it during the celebration dinner with Mom and Dad, and Miyu and her mom.

"What's wrong?" Miyu asks while our parents talk.

I swallow some mashed potatoes—with gravy this time. "I'm sick of the secrets. I have to tell them or I'm going to go crazy. Tango Kaitlin wouldn't be afraid to confess."

"Tango Kaitlin? Is that like your superhero alter ego?"

"Something like that." When I was skating today, I felt I could do anything and be anyone. I wasn't afraid of placing last or worrying what everyone would think of me. It felt good.

Miyu glances at her mom. "How about if we disappear for a few minutes?" She pushes her plate away. "Hey, Mom, I just remembered I left my gloves at the rink. We have to get them."

"Okay, we'll go after dinner," Mrs. Murakami says.

"We have to go now." Miyu's voice rises like this is a serious glove emergency. "They're my lucky gloves!"

A crease appears over Mrs. Murakami's eyes. "I didn't know you had lucky gloves."

"I need them! It's just down the street. We can come right back."

"Go on," Mom says. "I understand lucky gloves. We'll order you dessert."

Mrs. Murakami sighs and picks up her purse. "All right."

As soon as they're gone, I channel Tango Kaitlin—minus the flirty eyes. "So, I wanted to talk to you guys about something." I cross my fingers under the table. I can do this. I've done so much in these past two months I never thought I could, so this shouldn't be that hard. Still, it feels like the room just got ten degrees warmer.

"That sounds serious," Dad says.

Mom frowns. "Are you finally going to admit you didn't drive the Zamboni into the wall?"

Oh, yeah. Make that another secret I'm still keeping.

"Um . . . I was there, but Braedon was driving."

"I knew it." Mom slaps the table with her hand. "I'm going to talk to Greg."

"No! I mean, Braedon's going to talk to him, so you don't have to do anything. I was still part of it, and I know I should've left, so no matter what happens to Braedon, I still owe the rink."

Dad nods. "That's a very grown-up attitude."

I look at my plate. "There's something else." I don't look up, but I can picture Mom's face. "So . . . you know that party?"

"Yes," Mom says. "How could we forget it?"

"That was kind of my idea."

My parents just look at me for a second without saying anything. I cross the fingers on my other hand.

"I thought Braedon was in charge of that," Mom says.

“Right, didn’t he withdraw from the competition to pay for the room?” Dad adds.

“Yeah. He admitted to it before I could. The assistant manager wanted to kick out the entire club, but Braedon took the blame for everything before I could stop him.” I glance up.

Mom’s face is unreadable.

But Dad smiles a little. “That was gallant.”

I try not to laugh. It’s exactly the word I’d thought of.

“You organized that? Invited everyone? Made that nice video?” Mom asks. Greg had made sure to tell everyone’s parents all the details of the party.

“Technically Braedon invited everyone, but I came up with the idea and made the video. I wanted all the other skaters to see that we’re just normal, fun people. And to maybe actually like us.” I brace myself for another lecture.

“Hmm. Well, it seems to have worked,” she says.

“It . . . what?”

Now she’s smiling a little. “I should’ve known you had it in you somewhere, Kaitlin. You’re my daughter, through and through.”

I don’t know what to say, but I think of how Mom almost always gets what she wants. She’s never afraid to say exactly how she feels, or do what needs to be done to make something happen. Maybe I am more like her than I thought.

"If you hadn't come up with that idea and had the guts to see it through, you wouldn't have had all that support behind you when you skated," Mom says.

Okay, that's not the reaction I expected at all. But there's more. And I know Mom won't be happy about this one. "So . . . remember when you dropped me off at dance class and went to the grocery? I kind of didn't go. To the class, I mean. I went to Burger Hut instead."

Dad covers his mouth. It almost looks like he's about to laugh. Probably because he'd pick eating burgers over dancing any day.

"So that's what Jill was talking about. You went by yourself?" Mom asks.

I look at my hands. "With Braedon."

Mom makes this I-knew-that-boy-was-trouble sound.

"But it was my choice," I say before she can blame him. "I didn't have to go. I'll pay you back with my birthday money for the class I missed. And I'm sorry you're disappointed in me."

Dad reaches across the table and covers my hand with his. "We aren't disappointed in you."

I check his eyes for that Disappointed Dad look. It's not there.

"You've made some poor choices," Mom says. "But you're learning from them, and that's what's important."

Oookay. I thought Mom would freak out and start lecturing me about responsibility and peer pressure and wasted opportunity.

"In fact," Dad says, "we have a surprise for you."

"A surprise grounding?" I don't know what else they could possibly be thinking of.

Mom laughs. "No, that would be an awful surprise. What have you wanted more than anything—aside from going to Nationals?"

That's easy. To go to school. But there's no way. . . .

Dad's got his goofiest Dad grin in place, and Mom can't stop tapping her fork on the tablecloth.

"Not . . ." I'm almost afraid to say it out loud. What if they were thinking back to when I was five and all I really wanted was a purple pony?

"School!" The word practically explodes out of Mom's mouth. "We enrolled you in Grove Middle School, starting in January. Right after Nationals."

I give a little shriek and leap up to hug them both. "Really? This January?"

"You bet," Dad says.

"Of course, you'll need to keep up your training," Mom adds.

"I will, I promise. After all, I'm going to Nationals!" I sit down because the whole restaurant is staring at the crazy girl in the bright blue Fallton jacket who won't stop hugging her parents. "What made you change your mind?"

"You've had a rough couple of months," Mom says. "A few weeks ago I would've said no way. But you've grown so much since then. You're assertive and you've come through something that would've made most people quit the sport. You're coming out of your shell." She pauses. "I'm proud of you, Kaitlin."

"Me too," Dad says.

I don't even know what to say. I'm beginning to wonder if aliens abducted my real mother, because this Mom isn't reacting at all the way I thought she would. I think of Addison's mom, and I realize how different mine is—and how lucky I am to have her.

So I say the only thing I can. "Thank you."

"Now, we'll have to set up a time for you to take a tour, meet your teachers, and all of that. I'll talk to the principal when we get back home." Mom pulls out her phone and starts typing away. Probably one of the gazillion reminders she sets for herself every day.

"Mom, I think I should do that. Set up the tour and all, I

mean." Old Kaitlin would never in a million years say something like that. Tango Kaitlin, however, is totally brave enough to call a new school and arrange everything she needs to start.

Mom smiles. "Of course."

"So there's one more . . ." I trail off when I see Dad's face. "What's wrong?"

"Is this another confession?" he asks.

"There can't possibly be anything else," Mom says. She tilts her head and frowns a little. "Right?"

I swallow my climbing-out-of-Miyu's-window admission. Tango Kaitlin's done enough damage tonight. "No. Just wanted to see if you guys were ready to order dessert."

When I admit my part in the party to Greg, I brace myself for the worst. How could he want to be my coach when I embarrassed him and then let Braedon take the fall?

"*You* did that?" he says in amazement.

"Yeah. I'm really sorry. I almost got the entire club kicked out," I say.

"Huh." He's looking at me like I'm somebody else.

"You're not mad at me?"

Greg shakes his head. "You should've asked me and your parents so we could've done everything the right way. And you should have thrown the party after the competition was finished, but I think it's all worked out for the best. I've never heard so much cheering for our skaters. And that's all thanks to you." Then he smiles.

I guess he's okay with Tango Kaitlin too.

"So all of this stuff . . . the party, the Zamboni, even Praterville . . . that's how you finally skated to the music," he says. "You were able to draw on feelings you'd actually experienced. When you performed at Regionals, you moved with passion and fire."

I remember what the girl I met at the party said about pairing real emotions with her music. "So, I should get into a bunch of trouble before every competition?" I give him a mischievous smile.

"Don't you dare. But you can draw on those feelings anytime you want." He taps my CD against the palm of his hand. "Now, enough talking. We need to get on with practicing for Nationals. You only have three months."

As I take my starting position, Braedon skates by and grins at me. And when the music starts, Tango Kaitlin knows exactly what to do.

Acknowledgments

Hey, you. Yeah, you, the kid reading this book. THANK YOU!! Without you, this book wouldn't exist and I'd have to tell stories to my plants. Come visit me online at www.gailnall.com. I'd love to hear from you!

Breaking the Ice wouldn't be more than words on a computer if it weren't for the amazing team at Aladdin, especially Annie Berger, who took a chance on my little skating book, and Amy Cloud, who jumped in with so much enthusiasm. Kaitlin's story is so much better because of you both. A huge thanks to everyone at Aladdin who touched this book in any way! I also owe cake of every flavor and shape and size (and maybe some black olive and pineapple pizza, too) to superagent Julia A. Weber, for all of her business smarts and editorial advice and cheerleading.

A writer doesn't get very far without the help of other writers. And I've been so, so, so lucky to find some seriously amazing and talented writer friends. To Jen Malone, Stefanie Wass, Heather Brady, and Manju Howard, beta-readers extraordinaire; to Gretchen Kelley, Sara O'Bryan Thompson,

Mel Conklin, Dee Romito, Abby Cooper, Mike Winchell, Krista Van Dolzer, and Brenda Drake, for words of wisdom and encouragement; to the LL&N critique group, for reading all the bits and pieces—Charles Suddeth, Laura Stone, Amy Williamson, Anne Howard, and David Jarvis; to Team Weber, for constant support and virtual confetti cannons—Amanda Burckhard, E. M. Caines, Rebecca Hackett, Robin Hall, Andrea Jackson, Precy Larkins, and L. S. Murphy; to the ever-amazing MG Beta Readers, for being there every step of the way; to the Fearless Fifteeners—I couldn't ask for a better group of debut authors!; to everyone in SCBWI Midsouth, particularly Genetta Adair, Candie Moonshower, Rae Ann Parker, Courtney Stevens, and Kristin O'Donnell Tubb, for welcoming a newbie writer with open arms, encouragement, and big smiles—this book wouldn't be a book if I hadn't joined SCBWI; and finally, to the wider kidlit writing community on Twitter and the Blue Boards: you all are the best! I wish I could name more names, but it's generally accepted that the acknowledgments should be shorter than the actual book.

To Loismarie Van Ormer and Susan Caudill, for never letting me forget to bend my knees or keep my shoulders back; to Bob Farmer and Alpine Ice Arena, for being a second home during my younger years; to Darryl Coffelt, for the Zamboni ride and answering all my Zamboni-related questions, and Brian Farmer, for the Zamboni manual and enthusiasm; to the Louisville Figure Skating Club, Louisville Skating Academy, US Figure Skating, and the Ice Skating Institute, for simply existing and helping young (and old!) skaters' dreams come true every day.

To my friends Whitney Powell (thanks a million for the tango help!), Jennie Cole, Frances Adams, Marife Bautista, Margie Wise, and to everyone at St. John Center, for keeping me sane. I love you all, and I owe you more than I can ever give.

And, most importantly, to my family: Mom, for telling me I could do anything I wanted; Dad, for always making me laugh; Cheryl, for endless hours acting out *Little House on the Prairie*, Sweet Valley Twins, and the Saddle Club; to Joel, Linda, Mike and Joann, Lisa and David, for all of the love and support; and finally, to Eva, my inspiration.

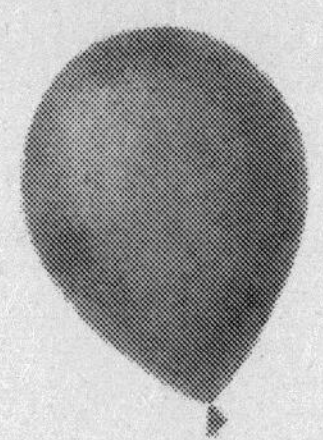

Turn the page for a peek at
Gail Nall and Jen Malone's

YOU'RE INVITED

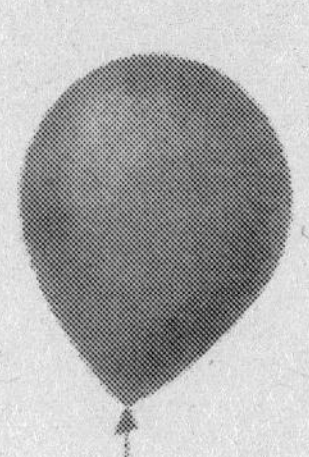

1

TODAY'S TO-DO LIST:

☐ sync watch with Mom's

☐ buy seasick medicine

☐ pack backup bridesmaid dresses

When I peer over the boat railing, it's not like I actually expect mermaids and mermen to be bobbing in the ocean below me. Buuuuuut then again, I wouldn't put anything past my mom. If her client wants a *Little Mermaid* wedding, her client gets a *Little Mermaid* wedding, no detail spared.

My pocket buzzes and I slide my phone out.

Plz check on photog. Thx.

I weave my way through the rows of chairs sliding back and forth on the deck. The one thing Mom doesn't control on wedding days is the weather, and today isn't exactly offering ideal sailing conditions. I hope the bride has less wobbly legs than Ariel.

"Excuse me, sir, um, are you okay?" I ask a man hanging over the boat's side.

The three cameras hanging from his neck smack against his back as he straightens. Uh-oh. He does *not* look so hot. He mumbles something under his breath and I shake my head.

"Sorry. I didn't catch that. Would you mind repeating?" I ask, using my most polite voice. Mom's trained me well.

He stares at me for a second, then screams, "I SAID I'M A LITTLE SEASICK!"

Okay, so "please repeat" does not mean "scream at your highest possible volume," but I'm kind of used to the vendors treating me differently. They think just because I'm only twelve, I'm not capable of the same things a normal wedding coordinator's assistant is.

They would be wrong.

I plant my feet hip-width apart for balance and get straight to business. "I have a seasick bracelet you can wear on your wrist, and if you give me five minutes, I can grab some of the motion-sickness medicine I packed in my emergency kit. I also have a little sister who's a pretty decent photographer, if you're okay with her using one of your cameras. She could stand at the railing and grab the shots of the bride arriving by dinghy while you wait for the medicine to kick in."

His face was already turning green when I mentioned the dinghy, but he adds a look of horror to that. "I can't allow a *child* to photograph this wedding!"

I consider telling him kids can do *lots* of stuff every bit as well as any grown-up, but then the boat rolls over a large swell, and with the way he clutches at his stomach, I don't have the heart.

Between sucking in big breaths of fresh air, he says, "My assistant will take all the important shots of the bridal party. Tell your sister she can help by getting photos of the guests."

And just like that Izzy lands herself an assignment. Ick. She'll be totally annoying and gloaty about this all week now.

But the client comes first, and my job is to save the day. Good thing I really love my job, and even more important, good thing I'm really excellent at my job, even if certain people (cough, *Mom*, cough) hardly bother to acknowledge it.

Half the time she doesn't even know I'm solving a crisis, like making sure the waiter knows the groom's grandmother is allergic to wheat or scuffing up the waxed dance floor before anyone has an epic wipeout. My job is to keep things off *her* plate, and that's what I do. Always.

My phone buzzes again. On wedding days, no one besides Mom would dare text me.

Sure enough:

All handled w/photog? Bride arrival in 6 min.

Not five minutes. Not ten minutes. *Six* minutes. And you could set your clock by Mom's schedule, too. I tell the photographer I'll be right back and race below-decks to the staging area where all the various wedding paraphernalia is located, alongside my sister, Isabelle. She's sitting on top of the backup wedding gown with her face stuck in a book.

"Izzy, you're gonna get that completely wrinkled! The bride is gonna need to wear that if she gets something on her real dress."

"Relax, Sadie. You know Mom would never let anything happen to the actual dress."

"Well, what if . . . what if a wave crashes into the dinghy on the bride's way out to the boat? How do you think Mom's gonna prevent that?"

"Umbrellas." Izzy points out the tiny round window of the cabin at a wooden dinghy motoring toward us. It's too far to make out faces, but there are definitely umbrellas bobbing along either side of one of the figures. Mom thinks of ev-er-y-thing.

I scramble back from the window and pull my sister to her feet. "Hurry up! The photographer's sick and his assistant needs your help getting shots."

Izzy squeals with excitement and follows me up the stairs. She's practically bouncing by the time we reach him. I think getting her to stop is the main reason he hands off what is probably a ridiculously expensive camera to a ten-year-old so quickly. His other hand reaches for the Dramamine and the seasick band I hold out.

He swallows the pill and then takes my advice to focus on the horizon. You don't grow up in Sandpiper Beach, North Carolina, without learning the best ways to get your sea legs.

"Izzy, head over to where the guests are and grab some shots of them watching the bridal party arrive," I instruct.

She answers with a "You're not the boss of me," but at least she does what I ask as I run to make sure the groom is in place. My favorite thing about weddings is also my least favorite: everything happens at once.

But this one is a success so far. Okay, so maybe the wedding party has a hard time getting out of their dinghies since their bridesmaid dresses have sewn-on mermaid tails, and it's true that the photographer throws up the Dramamine before it can even reach his stomach. But you can tell the bride and groom are really in love, what with the way he makes googly eyes at her as she comes down the aisle to a steel-drum version of "Kiss the Girl."

Mom slides into place beside me.

"Thanks for your help today," she whispers while giving me a squeeze around my waist.

Now it's my turn to glow. Ever since Dad died and Mom started her wedding-planning company, she's been totally preoccupied with her business. I get the whole I-need-a-distraction-from-the-grief thing, but it's almost like she wants a distraction from me and Izzy, too. So the times when she actually notices me, it's like . . . magic. Like it used to be.

I don't have that much time to savor the feeling,

though, because I need to get going on my next task. As the couple exchanges vows, I sneak belowdecks and creep over to the cage of the shaggy sheepdog who belongs to one of the bridesmaids and just *happens* to match the one in *The Little Mermaid*. I mean, what are the odds?

"You ready for your big entrance, Fake Max?" I ask, checking his collar to make sure the pouch containing the wedding rings is fastened securely around the buckle. I don't know what this dog's name is, but I've watched *The Little Mermaid* alongside my note-taking Mom enough over the past few months to know Prince Eric's dog is named Max, so it will have to do.

He woofs at me and plants a sloppy kiss on my cheek. Ick. This job has a ton of occupational hazards, and now I can add dog slobber to the list. I secure his leash and lead him above, sneaking him around the back of the seated wedding guests.

The minister smiles at the happy couple and asks, "Do you have the rings?"

That's my cue.

And then . . . it happens.

A big plop of seagull doo-doo drops from the sky and lands directly on my head, dribbling greenish-yellowish-whitish goop down my cheek. When I scream, everyone swivels as one to face me. I freeze, horrified by both my interruption and the super-slimy, super-gross stuff sliding down toward my neck.

The groom drops the bride's hands.

I drop the dog's leash.

Fake Max goes tearing off in wild circles around the deck, barking like crazy at the circling seagull, who looks like he's lining up target practice with the top of my head again.

"Grab him!" Mom screams as Fake Max pulls up at my ankles, panting hard. But I don't grab him, because:

1) I can't take my eyes from the seagull, who looks suspiciously like he's about to dive-bomb straight for my head, and

2) I'm thinking about how I'm going to use a printed program to remove bird poop from my hair.

Fake Max is eyeing the gull too, and when the bird swoops low, the dog jumps into the air at him. Of course he misses, since his shaggy fur is probably completely covering his eyes. Landing, he then tears off across the deck in hot pursuit of the bird, who I would swear is laughing more than screeching. Fake Max runs, pauses, and then jumps, chasing the seagull straight off the back of the boat, his four furry legs still running through the air, as he drops to the water below.

His owner shrieks, "SHEP!" and shuffle-runs across the deck in her mermaid dress. She doesn't even hesitate at the railing, just goes right up and over, tumbling into the water after her dog.

"Bridesmaid overboard!" someone calls, and several men run to the stern, one carrying a life preserver.

I rush to help, but when the man with the life preserver swings it behind him before heaving it into the water, I have to dodge out of the way. I stumble back and straight into the box the steering wheel is mounted on, where my elbow connects hard with a button.

KA-BAAM! POP! POW! BANG! BOOM!

The entire ten-minute fireworks display planned for the end of the reception explodes at one time from the barge on the starboard side of us.

Activated by me.

I stand frozen in place again, my wide eyes locked with my mother's, as a group of tuxedo-wearing men haul a dripping mermaid/bridesmaid/whatevermaid and her soggy dog out of the water. At least the pouch with the rings is still attached to his collar.

But that thing I said about being really good at my job? Maybe not so much today.

Mom likes to borrow a theater saying when she talks about her "event philosophy": The show must go on. I'm pretty sure she's never had to apply it quite like this before. I clean up belowdecks and then hang back as much as I can, trying to help without getting in the way. Mom barely even acknowledges me as she rushes around doing wedding-planner stuff, but when she does catch my eye, I see the way her lips tug down into a frown. Each time it happens, my stomach has that hollow feeling you get when you just know you are so completely in for it once everyone else leaves.

The ceremony resumes where it left off and is pretty uneventful except for Max/Shep shaking himself dry at the top of the aisle during the you-may-now-kiss-the-bride part. Luckily for us, once people get over the shock—and after Mom changes the bridesmaid into a backup mermaid dress (only two sizes too small)—things start looking up (not for me, but at least for the guests). The bridesmaid calls her mom to come to the marina, and we send the horrible-smelling wet dog back to the mainland on the dinghy. He's joined by the still-puking photographer.

By the last toast of the night, the video of the entire incident, which one of the groomsmen wasted no time posting to YouTube, has 244,365 hits. By the last dance at sunset, the bride and groom have agreed to detour to Wilmington on their way to the honeymoon in order to discuss their "hilarious wedding disaster" on the local morning show.

All's well that ends well? Not where Mom's concerned, I'm guessing. The chug of the departing dinghy signals the official end of the reception. The only people left on the boat now, besides me and Mom, are the caterers cleaning up and Izzy, who's gone back to her book down below.

Mom crosses the deck and points me into a chair near the giant Prince Eric ice sculpture.

"I'm so sorry, Mom," I say before she can get a word out.

She sighs and reaches for my hand. "I know you are, baby, and I understand how it happened."

Her smile is the kind that doesn't go all the way into her eyes, which are a little sad-looking. I stare back into them as she says, "On the other hand, I have the reputation of my business to think about, and I have to put that first."

Ahead of me?

I drop my eyes to my lap. Mom sighs again. "Sweetness, maybe twelve is just too young to be handling everything I've asked of you. Maybe we need to rethink things a little bit."

Wait a minute. Am I getting fired? By my own *mother*? This cannot be happening.

"You've been a huge help to me, Sadie. You know that. But this mistake is going to cost the company thousands of dollars after I refund the bride's dad for the fireworks show he paid for. Plus we lose any referrals that bride could have given us. I just hope she doesn't mention my company by name on television Monday morning."

She tucks me under her arm and gives me a squeeze. I keep my body stiff when she says, "I'm not mad, Sades. It's my fault for giving you so much responsibility. Summer's just starting. You should spend it doing kid stuff. Fun stuff. Not dealing with all this stress."

Does she not remember the whole reason I started working with her is because I DO find it fun? Well, at first it was just because it was a chance to be with Mom, but it turns out I'm really good at it . . . most days. I'm the one who came up with the idea for the ice sculpture to match the statue in the movie. And it was me who tracked down the sheet music for "Kiss the Girl" for the wedding band. I love coming up with fun details to make the weddings memorable and I *thought* Mom loved it too. She's always going on about what a huge help I am to her.

I didn't notice anyone *else* thinking to bring a blender for that groom who'd had emergency dental surgery the morning of the wedding, so he could still have some wedding cake. Or finding weights to clip onto the bridesmaids' dresses' hems when we had an outdoor wedding on the beach during a super-windy day. And, I mean, it's not like I haven't made some little mistakes at a wedding before. There was the time I accidentally left with the keys to the reception site and the florist couldn't get in early to do the centerpieces. But I rode my bike over as fast as I could the second she called. Maybe tonight's was a little more . . . severe, but in the past Mom's always understood that events might have wrinkles.

It stinks to be unappreciated, but what's even worse

is being entirely invisible. Which is exactly what I'll be if she fires me. I'll fade back into the wallpaper like before.

I nod hard against Mom's chest so she won't catch on that I'm trying not to let the tears spill over. We're interrupted by the caterer, who needs her to sign some form, which leaves me free to slide my phone from my pocket and scroll through all my emoticons until I find the tiny pair of bat wings. I type it into a group text to my three best friends.

There. Bat signal sent.

It cheers me up a tiny bit to picture all of them heading for their bikes (or golf cart, for Lauren, depending on where she is at the marina) and pointing them to our Bat Cave. Well, our Bat Boat, if we're being technical.

I stand, cross the deck, and yell down to Izzy that I'm catching the next dinghy shuttle to shore. As I board the tiny boat, the last thing I hear is someone from the catering staff humming "Part of Your World" as she cleans up. Too bad my chance to be part of Mom's world exploded alongside those fireworks.